Feenin' for a Real One 3

Tina J

Copyright 2017

More Books by Tina J

A Thin Line Between Me & My Thug 1-2
I Got Luv for My Shawty 1-2
Kharis and Caleb: A Different kind of Love 1-2
Loving You is a Battle 1-3
Violet and the Connect 1-3
You Complete Me
Love Will Lead You Back
This Thing Called Love
Are We in This Together 1-3
Shawty Down to Ride For a Boss 1-3
When a Boss Falls in Love 1-3
Let Me Be The One 1-2
We Got That Forever Love
Ain't No Savage Like The One I got 1-2
A Queen & Hustla 1-2 (collab)
Thirsty for a Bad Boy 1-2
Hasaan and Serena: An Unforgettable Love 1-2
We Both End Up With Scars
Caught up Luvin a beast 1-3
A Street King & his Shawty 1-2
I Fell for the Wrong Bad Boy 1-2 (collab)
Addicted to Loving a Boss 1-3
All Eyes on the Crown 1-3
I Need that Gangsta Love 1-2 (collab)
Still Luvin' a Beast 1-2
Creepin' With The Plug 1-2
I Wanna Love You 1-2
Her Man, His Savage 1-2
When She's Bad, I'm Badder 1-3
Marco & Rakia 1-3
Feenin' for a Real One 1-3

Previously...

Pierce

"Where you at? Something happened to Ingrid?" I called Rebel for the tenth time. Her phone went to voicemail and it only pissed me off.

"Did you get her?" Cason asked. Two days have gone by and I haven't heard from my girl. I was definitely worried and had no way of finding her.

"Nah. I have no idea where she is or how to get in touch with her."

"Pierce, she's ok." Ingrid said. She woke up yesterday and cried most of the day, after finding out she was pregnant.

"How you know? She called?"

"No, but this is her second to last job. When she goes, sometimes she shuts her phone off." I couldn't really disagree because the last job she went on, she cursed me out for

4

allowing Shayla to kiss me. She wouldn't speak to me for a couple weeks.

"I need to meet who this boss is because she won't be taking that last job."

"I told her the same thing but her boss is not giving her a choice."

"What you mean?" She went to speak but my phone went off. I saw it was a message from Shayla and once I opened the text, my anger went from zero to a hundred, real quick. I walked over to Ingrid.

"Who is this?" She took the phone from my hand and stared. There was a photo of Rebel and some dude, sitting in a restaurant. It looked like they were about to kiss in the picture. You couldn't tell who he was because of the hat.

"I don't know."

"Oh. I'm gonna find out."

"Pierce, its not what you think." Ingrid said on my way out the door. I stopped and stared.

"You know about this?" She tried to speak and another picture came through. This one was her going into a hotel. A hotel, I knew all too well.

"Not everything. She was supposed to tell you about her job. Pierce, please don't hurt her."

"I can't make promises. I told her not to cheat on me."

"Yo, what's going on?" Cason asked and stood up.

"I'm about to kill her."

"SHIT! Ma, stay here with her. I'll send Sam up here to watch over y'all." He kissed his girl and I heard him on the phone with Sam.

On the drive to find Rebel, all I could think of was, if she fucked another nigga and how I just told her, I loved her. How could she repeat those same words and be in a hotel with someone else? I know, Shayla was having a ball sending me those photos. Especially; since she's been telling me over the last few days in messages, that my girl ain't shit and a ho. I ignored her because she was hateful but who knew, she may be telling the truth?

I parked at the hotel and became even more angry, when I spotted her car. How the hell she claim to be going out of town and right here, in Manhattan? Cason, was right behind me. I walked up to the receptionist and asked if she saw Rebel. She said there was no one with that name in the hotel. I showed her a photo and she said a woman, resembling her, just walked in five minutes ago. I told her it was my sister and I needed to know which room she was in because there was a death in the family. Once she gave it to me, I handed her a fifty.

The entire ride up the elevator, my heart was racing. I could hear my cousin telling me to calm down and hear what she has to say. Nothing was processing right now and he knew it, which is why he stopped me when we got off, on the floor. The room was all the way down the hall because it was a penthouse suite. I looked at him, stepped back and shot the handle off the door. Thank goodness for silencers. The music was so loud they didn't even know, I was there. What I saw next, made me lose my fucking mind. Rebel, was sitting on some guys lap, allowing him to kiss on her neck. His back was to me and she had her eyes closed. I don't know, if I were mad

7

she was here, or the fact she seemed to be enjoying it. I put my gun on her forehead.

"You got one motherfucking second to explain."

"PIERCE!" She shouted and made the guy jump. I became even more angry, when I saw the guy is someone, who worked for me on Ohio. What the fuck is he doing in New York and why is he with my girl? This is De Ja Vu like a motherfucker. He is one of my top money makers too, which is really making me question why he's here.

"Boss, what you doing here? And why you have a gun, on my company?" I knew then, he had no idea who she was.

"Leave Jason."

"What the fuck is going on?"

"I'm not gonna say it again." I kept my eyes trained on Rebel and Cason, told Jason to bounce. Once he left, I could see the tears rolling down her face.

"Baby, let me explain." I checked my gun to make sure every bullet was in there.

"I told you not to cheat on me, right?"

"Pierce, please."

"RIGHT!" She shook her head yes.

"Cason, please get him."

"Don't bring him into this because if you were Ingrid, he'd be doing the same thing."

"Sure would."

"Pierce, let me explain. I wasn't going to cheat on you."

"That's not what the fuck, I walked in on. The nigga was kissing on your neck, feeling on your body and not once, did you make him get up."

"I know, but.-" I kept hearing her stall. I lifted my gun up and pointed it at her head. Something told me to look down and I never noticed before but she definitely had a stomach. I mean it wasn't huge but it was there.

"Are you fucking pregnant?" She put her head down.

"Whose is it?" She looked at me and her face turned up. I didn't even wanna know and let my finger pull the trigger back.

BOOM! BOOM! And just like that, her body dropped.

9

Rebel

"Sway, who is this dude you have me meeting and why do you want my phone turned off?" The guy, I was originally supposed to meet had a death in the family, which is why I was able to stick around when Ingrid brought Miracle home. I knew nothing about this person he was sending me on a date with.

"Someone gave me his information. He's a dude from outta state and he's coming in for a wedding. I need you to reel him in."

"Sway, I only have two jobs left. I hope you know, I'm counting this as one of them."

"Yea. Yea. Just get dressed and show up at the wedding. I don't need to school you on how to work your magic but you know what to do." I hung up, prepared myself for this bullshit and left to handle my business.

That was two days ago and now, I'm standing here crying because Pierce found out and had his gun pointed at me. I wasn't really concerned with that as much as, I was with him asking whose child it is. I know shit may look suspect right

10

now but I damn sure never allowed a man to touch me, during this pregnancy. I'm surprised he didn't realize it sooner. But then again, I am big boned and the doctor said I may not show right away. He also said, when I do, I'm gonna blow up.

I looked up when he asked about my child and stared into the eyes of Shayla, pointing her gun at me. Cason nor Pierce knew she was there because she hid behind the door. She had to have been in here, before me and dude got in. How the hell she did it, is beyond me. When I turned my face up, she let off a shot and another one. My body hit the ground hard and I felt blood gushing out. I had no idea where and all I could hear is Pierce telling me, I was gonna be ok. I thought he would be happy I got hit but the tears coming down his face, falling onto mine, only proved he still loved me.

"I'm sorry Pierce. I swear, I didn't cheat on you. If I make it, I'll explain everything."

"Don't talk Reb. The ambulance is on the way." I could feel him applying pressure on my chest and the other hand was on my leg. The pain was so bad, all I wanted to do was sleep and make it go away.

"Stay awake, Reb. You can't go to sleep."

"Pierce, its hurting too bad. Let me just sleep until the people get here."

"NO! Don't go to sleep.

"Pierce, please. I just want the pain to go away."

"FUCK! Cason where is the ambulance? Shit, they're taking too long." I could hear him yelling, as my body became weaker.

"I love you Pierce."

"Reb, stop talking like that. You're gonna be fine." I tried to respond but my eyes closed.

****

I woke up to beeping noises and instantly grabbed my stomach. I felt a hand on top of mine and as bad as, I wanted it to be Pierce, it was my mom. She gave me a loving look and kissed my forehead. Without saying a word, she lifted the nurses button and pressed it. I felt her tears on my arm as she rubbed it.

The doctor came in, checked my vital and slowly removed the tube from my mouth. It hurt and I coughed up a lot of green shit. He then asked the nurse to come assist him in removing the catheter. That too, hurt coming out. The blood pressure cuff started squeezing me and I could hear the machines going crazy. It wasn't because he was hurting me but because I saw my child on the screen. Evidently, one of the beeping noises was the baby monitor on my stomach and after he took the catheter out, he did a quick ultrasound for me. I was four months, two weeks and three days, from what the picture said. I was so happy and all I wanted to do was call Pierce.

"Ma'am, you should relax." The doctor said when I tried reaching for the hospital phone.

"I have to call my boyfriend." My mom gave me a sad look.

"What? Is he ok?" My voice was still hoarse but they could hear me.

"Can you excuse us doctor?" He nodded and stepped out. My mom sat on the side of the bed and grabbed my hand.

"Honey, Pierce is in jail."

"WHAT?" She patted my hand.

13

"When the cops found you in the hotel room, he had your blood all over him and some chick told the cops she witnessed him shoot you."

"But he didn't."

"Rebel, the door was opened and there's a camera showing him pointing a gun at you."

"No. No. No." I took the covers off my leg and almost passed out, from the amount of pain in my chest. I lost my breath and my mom had to yell for a doctor to come in.

"What happened?"

"I just told her." He asked me if I were ok and stood there until my machines were back to normal.

"I need to see him. Who's the cop that arrested him? Ma, please call Cason to get him out."

"He's been trying but the captain said, since the media is all over it, they had to wait."

"I have to see him." I grabbed my stomach because it started balling up.

"Ma'am, you need to calm down or you're going to lose the baby." I laid back and the tears cascaded down my face.

"Its my fault."

"Huh?" The doctor had a sad look on his face.

"If he wasn't coming there to get me, he'd never be in jail. I was doing one of my last jobs and.-"

"Rebel you can't blame yourself. Whoever this woman is told the police, he tried to kill you because he found you with another man. I thought you were in love with Pierce. Were you cheating on him?"

"Yes and no." She gave me a weird look.

"Where's Ingrid?"

"Oh Rebel, you've missed a lot."

"A lot of what?"

"Cason told me, some woman named Rose tried to kill her. She drug her body half way down the street and almost made her lose the baby."

"BABY?"

"Yea. She's pregnant. I think he said two months."

"Oh my God. I'm so happy for her."

"Everyone is. Oh hey!" She said and in walked Ms. Edna, Pierce's mom."

"I'll be back." She shut the door behind her.

"How are you Rebel?" She came on the other side of me.

"I really don't know. I just woke up and found out my man is in jail behind false accusations. I can't even talk to him and.-" She passed me a phone and took a seat on the chair.

"Hello."

"You can give the phone back to my mom." I heard him say.

"Pierce, are you ok? When are you coming home?"

"I just needed to know you were ok. Don't worry about anything I have going on and when you deliver, I want a test."

"WHAT?" I yelled, which wasn't too loud with no voice. His mom stood and took the phone from me. She said a few things to him and hung up.

"Just ask me."

"Rebel, I'm not here to judge you or your job occupation. I just want to know why you didn't tell him? Is this really my grandchild?"

"I know he found me in an uncompromising position but this is your grandchild. Ms. Edna, I never cheated on him; regardless of how it may look. I am in love with your son and the only reason I was there, is to finish the last two jobs on my contract. I didn't tell him because I refused to let him walk outta my life." She came close to me and pulled my chin up.

"Shayla told him, you work with some guy named Sway. And from what he tells me, Sway hires you to portray fake relationships with men. You bed them, make them vulnerable, and this guy comes in, robs and kills them. Were you trying to do that with my son?" I sat up the best I could.

"Ms. Edna, I was working with Sway before Pierce barged in my life. Sway has never mentioned Pierce or Cason to me. If he made plans to get at them, it isn't with me. Unless."

"Unless, what?"

"Unless, it's the last job he wanted me to do."

17

"What you mean?"

"He told me the last job would be the biggest ever and it involved two people. I didn't pay it any mind because he was always talking. Now that I think of it, Shayla asked me in the hospital if I wanted to help her get Pierce."

"What?"

"Yea, she said something about knowing how much money he had, from them being together previously. Oh my God! She's going to try and take Tiffany and all Peirce's money. Fuck! I have to get outta here."

"Calm down Rebel. Tell me everything and don't leave anything out."

I told her what went down with Sway from the first day we met. I left the governor's information out because he had nothing to do with anything. That reminds me. He owes me a favor and I think, its time to cash in on it. She asked me a lot of questions and I answered them the best I could. Her demeanor was the same and I couldn't tell if she was judging. When I finally finished, she picked the phone up and called someone to meet her up here.

"Does this Sway guy know about your relationship with Pierce?"

"Not that I know of. I never told him who I was with."

"It sounds like he already knew and used you, without you knowing."

"No. He wouldn't do me like that." She gave me the side eye.

"Oh, you better believe I'm gonna find out."

"Rebel, you're going to be discharged today and both your mom and I, want you to stay with her. Someone will be watching your house and wherever you go."

"Why?"

"Because we have reason to believe Shayla is working with him. She's going to do everything in her power to have you killed and make it look like an accident."

"What the fuck?"

"I told Pierce she was back for a reason. This has to be it." She said and opened the door. In walked Cason and Sam.

"About time you woke up. Got my cousin stressing out." I sucked my teeth.

"Aye! Don't even think about being mad at him for the sneaky shit he caught you doing."

"But.-"

"I don't wanna hear shit. Save it for whenever he feels like talking to you. Oh, and don't be stressing my girl out, either."

"Whatever." Him and Sam, stepped out while the doctor removed all the monitors from my stomach. I was surprised he discharged me but Cason said, there was a nurse coming to the house three times a day, to check on me for the next few days. I really hope, they find Shayla and Sway before me because if not, I'm taking both of their lives and I put that on everything.

Pierce

"No hard feelings Mr. Hill." The captain said and handed me my things.

"Its all good." I put my hat on, grabbed my shit and walked out the station. It felt good, to finally be outta there after three weeks. I was supposed to go in the county but the governor told them to keep me here in a cell, until things were sorted out. Evidently, the jail was overcrowded enough. Whether it's the truth or not, I could care less. I'm out and its all that matters now.

"Damn, you need a shave." Cason started the truck and pulled off. I never understood why he didn't use his personal driver as much.

"Hell yea. Take me to Selina's. Julius is the only one I like cutting my shit." He can be as gay as he wants but the nigga can't cut some hair.

He pulled up and the place was pretty packed. Cason, parked in the back where the employees do and we both got out. When we walked in, it seemed like every bitch was staring. Julius, made the chick get out his chair and another stylist went to help her. I sat down and let him do his thing. It felt good getting my shit washed and my face desperately needed to be fixed. By the time he finished, an hour had passed.

"How's Ingrid and your girl?" I snapped my neck and looked at him. He was best friends with Selina and she hated Rebel. Let alone, switched sides on Ingrid.

"What?" He shrugged his shoulders.

"Shit, Ingrid is cool as hell. Selina messed that up and I still don't know why she doesn't like the Rebel chick."

"Cason can tell you where Ingrid is. As far as, Rebel, I have no idea." I took the cape from around my neck.

"How you don't know where your girl at?" I chuckled.

"She ain't my girl no more." He put his hand on his chest being dramatic.

"It doesn't have anything with you wanting your shady ass baby mama, does it?"

"What the fuck you talking about?"

Cason had been to the jail with my mom everyday filling me in on the streets. Every time I asked where Shayla was, neither of them said a word. I may not be with Rebel any longer but my ex knew how I felt about her. When she took the shot and Rebel dropped in front of me, I felt what Cason did seeing Desi pass. I swore Reb was gone when she closed her eyes.

The EMT's came in right after and rushed her to the hospital. I tried to go but the cops came and said they had a witness saying, I did it. The camera showed me pointing my gun at her but I never pulled the trigger. Shit, I didn't have time to because Shayla did. Cason tried to run after Shayla but the stupid bitch ran down the steps and straight into the cops. She had to have it planned because they were there, way too fast.

The detectives tested my gun and all my bullets were still in there, so they knew I didn't do it. Of course, there was the asshole cop, who said Cason must've hidden it before they arrived. I never bothered to prove my innocence and let them think whatever. My lawyer tried hard to get me out but like the captain said, once the media got hold of it, the judge said I had to stay put.

"Word on the street is, she's tryna win you back or something." He said it in a non chalant way.

"Oh yea. Well, I'ma find out." I paid him and headed out back where I saw Cason going a few minutes ago. Him and Selina were going back and forth.

"Cason, how am I supposed to see my niece or nephew? Shit, I barely see the girls now."

"Not my problem. You should've thought about all that when you were talking shit. Then you bring it up at the hospital and entertained Rose at the courthouse. You had way too many chances to make shit right and blew it. I wouldn't even part my lips to ask her to forgive you." Selina stood there with her arms folded.

"I guess when you find out if the bitch is really pregnant by you, I can't see my cousin either." I shook my head.

"I don't give a fuck about your attitude but what you won't do, is disrespect my kids' mother."

"Evidently, she's everyone's baby's mama." Selina knew how to piss me off.

"I guess you can add your baby daddy to the list too then, huh?"

"He wouldn't dare fuck with her again."

"AGAIN?" Cason and I, both said at the same time.

"Yes again. I don't wanna talk about it." She waved us off.

"Don't underestimate what a nigga will do." I laughed at how mad she was getting.

"You don't even have a reason to be mad at Rebel and if you are, I'm sure its something from the past because you hold on to grudges." I moved past her and she grabbed Cason's arm.

"I wanna see Miracle and Kiyah." I knew she wouldn't ask me about Tiffany. My mom, is damn near at her mom's everyday with her. Oh, hell yea Tiffany is with us. I'll be damned if the bitch tries to leave with her again.

"I'll bring them by the house this weekend and Selina?" She was about to go in the shop.

"What?"

"Kiyah tells Ingrid everything. If she comes back and says you called Ingrid a name, that's your ass." She sucked her teeth and slammed the door.

"Kiyah snitches like that?"

"Man, she tells Ingrid everything. If I fart, she fucking tells." I fell out laughing.

He took me by my moms and Tiffany ran straight to me. I picked her up and all she talked about was Rebby. I loved the way Rebel took to my daughter and I hoped the baby she was pregnant with, is mine. I missed Shayla's entire pregnancy and the first two and a half years of her life.

In my heart, I feel the baby is mine but with everything that's happened, how can I not have doubts? I should've known from all the times she would get upset and be ready to cry over dumb shit. Even before she left for this last job, she said we had to talk. I bet that's exactly what she wanted to tell me.

"Hey!" Rebel came out the kitchen limping. Her stomach must've grown overnight because it was out there.

"Daddy, Rebby having my brother." She asked me to put her down and ran over to rub her stomach.

"What up?" I walked past her and went in the kitchen. It didn't take but a few minutes to hear the door slam and a car pull off.

"She's pregnant Pierce and any stress can harm the baby."

"Ma, I spoke." She folded her arms.

"I don't have anything to say."

"Pierce she's having your baby and you know it. I understand the job she was doing but think about it. Has she ever given you a reason to believe she'd cheat on you?" I didn't say a word. Rebel has always been upfront with me. It doesn't mean she'd mention cheating.

"Son, I would be hesitant to believe her too but I don't think she would've blamed a baby on you." I looked at her.

"She has her own money and doesn't need you or any man. Yet, you're the only one she's made a relationship with. Pierce, she gave up her job for you."

"Too late now." My mom rolled her eyes.

"Do you know when she got out the hospital she contacted the Sway dude. She told him, she doesn't care if he kills her and refuses to finish the last job." She came closer to me.

"That woman put her life on the line for you and all you say to her is, what up?" I stood there listening to my mom rip me a new one.

"I'll see her in a few days. Let me get my head right." I kissed her cheek and attempted to take my daughter. She said, she was staying with her grandmother.

I walked out with Cason and told him, I'd call tomorrow. I wanted to go home, take a hot shower and lay down in a real bed, which is exactly what I did. However; it didn't feel like home without Rebel. I threw my sneakers on, locked up and drove to her house. I used my key to get in, set the alarm and walked up the steps.

I opened the bedroom door and she was knocked out. The television was still on and so was the lamp, by her bed. There was a body pillow next to her and she had one of my shirts over it. I shook my head grinning and turned the TV and light off. I put my sneakers by the bed, took all my clothes off, except my t-shirt and boxers and got in with her. I moved the pillow and lifted her head to rest on my chest.

"Pierce? What are you doing here?" She lifted her head.

"We'll talk in the morning." I kissed her lips.

"Ok." She moved her leg on mine and placed my hand on her belly. I snatched my hand away when I felt something.

"Its just the baby kicking." She mumbled and fell right back to sleep with me doing the same.

****

I woke up the next day and Rebel was gone. I looked down at my phone and it was after 12. I guess, I was more tired than I thought. I slept at the jail but woke up more times then I care to admit. The piece of shit cot, was uncomfortable and I couldn't stop thinking about her. The surgery had her down for a few days and I was nervous on how she'd be after waking up.

I was happy when my mom called and told me she was ok. The captain never took my cell and even allowed Cason to bring me real food. I may not have been in the best place but I can't complain. I can complain about her not being here this morning. I wanted to know every fucking thing that's been going on. I heard my phone ringing and saw Cason calling me.

"Yea." I stood up to stretch.

"Where you at? I'm at your house and you ain't here."

"I stayed at Rebel's."

"Oh shit. Y'all made up?"

"Not really. I couldn't sleep without her." I wasn't ashamed to admit it.

"Pussy whipped ass."

"Oh, you can sleep without Ingrid?"

"Hell no but I ain't telling nobody that shit either." We both started laughing.

"I'm about to get dressed.

"Aight. I'll be here." I hung up, put my clothes on and left. The time will come for her to speak and when it does, she better not leave a damn thing out.

Shayla

"You stupid bitch. You were supposed to kill both of them."

WHAP! WHAP! Sway smacked and punched me over and over.

"Stop it Sway." I continued trying to block the hits but it was no use. His kicks were just as deadly. After another gruesome five minutes the beating finally stopped. My body was in so much pain, there's no way I could move.

"Get her incompetent ass outta here." He waved me off and one of the guards dragged me out. All I could think of was the day he did the same thing to the Rebel bitch. Here I thought it was funny, yet; suffering the exact same fate because her or Jason aren't dead.

The plan was for Rebel to meet Jason, get him back to the hotel and blindfold him. One of the other girls, were supposed to meet her in the room and sleep with him. I thought the bitch was lying when she said that's how Sway kept her from putting miles on her pussy. What I don't understand is why he lied about her just being someone he knew. Why didn't he just say he used to be or still is, in love with her?

Anyway, I switched places at the last minute with the chick because Sway got in his feelings about a phone call. Evidently, someone informed him that Rebel is indeed, Pierce's woman. I guess he knew she would never come back to him. He became irate and started telling me to get there fast and to kill both of them. Of course, I had no problem killing her and Jason is just a casualty of war.

Unfortunately, Pierce and Cason showed up and he was about to kill her. I stood there watching and couldn't wait for her to die. However; even when she cried, he had no remorse until he asked if she were pregnant. Once she said yes, I knew he wouldn't do it, which is why I came out the shadows and took those shots. I didn't have time to see her body drop because Cason was running behind me.

I hauled ass down those steps and he literally could reach out and touch me when I opened the door. And he would've, had the cops not been standing right there. Hell yea,

I sent a text to one of the girls when Rebel first showed up. I already had plans to pin her murder on Pierce. I knew he would go to jail and give me tons of money to take care of Tiffany. Who knew his ass would get out.

I'm not sure if he's back with the bitch because someone overheard him talking in the salon. He claimed she was no longer his girl. I guess after finding out the one you love is a ho; that love shit goes out the window. It did with us anyway and it was only one guy.

"I don't know why you bitches don't learn." The guard was dragging me and talking shit. There was so much blood leaking from my mouth, I couldn't respond if I wanted to.

"You would think after he beat some of the other girls to death, y'all would learn." He left me on the floor in a room and closed the door. *He beat the to death*? I said to myself. I needed to get outta here fast.

****

"About time you stopped acting hurt and brought your ass out the room." I looked at Sway like he lost his damn mind.

It's been two weeks since the beating took place and I still wasn't fully healed.

"Keep looking at me like that and see what happens." I sat at the table with the other girls and poured myself some orange juice. I looked around and wondered what the hell was I thinking coming down to Florida? I left my daughter and hadn't spoken to her or my mom since.

"Like I was saying before this bitch walked in." I rolled my eyes and was happy he didn't catch it.

"One of you, are gonna try and catch Pierce slipping."

"But how? Him and Cason are two of the hardest people to get. And with your best worker being in a relationship with him. It's going to be extremely hard." One of the girls said.

"And she knows a lot so I'm sure he's up on game." Another one spoke up.

"A nigga can never bypass new pussy. Therefore; I'ma need y'all to be on your A game. And you." He pointed to me.

"Go back to New York and put your ears to the streets."

"But he'll kill me if he sees me."

"Not my problem. You fucked up and let all of them live when you had all of them right there. You could've killed all four of them but your dumb ass ran."

"I want you ladies to pack and go with her. There's a room reserved for you and a rental car is available, as well. These are the spots you'll see then frequent the most. Get in where you fit in and don't fuck up. These niggas are gonna put me over the top and I don't need any fuck ups." He stared at me.

"Come here Shayla." He stood up and had me follow him in another room. I heard the door slam.

"Why you make me hit you?"

"Sway, I didn't make you do anything." He came behind me and let his arms go up my shirt. I hated to be touched by him right now but saying no, isn't an option.

"Bend over." His hand forced me to bend and his dick was in me, pounding away. The entire time he fucked me, I could tell his mind was elsewhere. I didn't even care. I just wanted it to be over and when it was, I pulled my clothes and walked out. I'm over his ass.

Rebel

As bad as I wanted to wake up in Pierce's arm the other day and explain what he saw, I had things to do and it starts with Jason. He's the guy Pierce caught me with and once he called him boss, I saw the hurt wash over his face. He probably assumed this was the same shit Shayla did to him a few years ago. It damn sure appeared that way but I had no clue of who he was or where he came from. However; I'm about to find out.

I called Jason and asked if he was coming to New York anytime soon and surprisingly he was. He was messing with some chick from out here. I asked if we could meet and at first, he was skeptical. With a boss like Pierce, I would be too but I needed to get more information from him.

I had to bite my lip when he came in. Jason is sexy as hell and put me in the mind frame of younger Shemar Moore. His swag and body are both on point. Any woman would be turned on by his sexy demeanor and I'm one of them.

"Hey!" I stood up and his eyes popped out his head.

"Yooooo. You didn't look like that last month." I grinned.

"I know. The doctor said, I could blow up at any time and I guess he was right." I rubbed my stomach and pointed for him to sit.

"I'm not about to get shot being here with you, am I?"

"No fool. He doesn't know about this meeting."

"Good." He picked the menu up.

"So. I asked you here because I needed to know, if you knew who I was and that Shayla was in the hotel room. Were you setting me up to be killed?"

"Answer her questions correctly and you won't die." I looked up and both Pierce and Cason were standing behind him. Of course, my stalker was there.

"Yo, what the hell is going on? I thought you said, he wouldn't be here."

"Do you know Pierce Hill?" I asked and he gave me a *Duh*, look.

"Then you should know his crazy ass will pop up anywhere, whether I invite him or not." I rolled my eyes.

"What are you doing here?" He grabbed a seat and Cason asked the waitress to come over with other menus.

"Y'all so fucking rude. What if this was a date?"

"Rebel, don't fucking push me." I waved him off.

"Now answer her questions."

"Look, I don't know what's going on. I come into town for a wedding and run into some dude named Sway. He said, he heard about me and wanted to hook up to work together." I did see him there. I assumed he was making sure, I came.

"Word!" Pierce seemed pissed.

"Yea. I told him, I'm good and kept it moving. He had some chick named Shayla try and talk to me but I wasn't biting. Then, I run into shorty here and she spit mad game. I was down and next thing I know, we exchange numbers and go out on a date. The night you came to the hotel is the first time we even touched. What's this about?"

"So, you have no idea who she is?" He pointed to me. I folded my arms. I know he asked for his own conscious.

"Ugh no. But from the looks of this right here and the shit at the hotel, I'd say she's your girl."

"Tsk. Yea right." I said.

"Yo, give us a minute." He snatched me up by my arm.

"Pierce, I can't move that fast and you're making my chest hurt." He moved me against the wall by the bathroom.

"I'ma make more than your fucking chest hurt if you don't stop playing."

"I'm not playing. You don't want me. Pierce, you were going to fucking kill me." I went to step off and he grabbed me.

"Reb."

"No, Pierce. I should've told you about my job but I was scared to lose you. Yes, you caught me in a fucked-up situation but I was never going to sleep with him. I was supposed to blindfold him and he was sending another woman in. I had no business allowing him to feel on me but I swear, I didn't kiss or sleep with him. I could never cheat on you." I left him standing there and went in the bathroom.

"Rebel, I'm sorry." I looked up.

"Why are you in here?"

"Because I don't want you upset. You're pregnant and I don't want anything to happen to you or the baby."

"Oh, the baby that may not be yours?" He didn't say anything. I scoffed up a laugh and went to the door. I turned around.

"You know Pierce, you're not the only one in the world who's been hurt in the past. I fucked up by not telling you but I would never accuse you of being my child's father, if you weren't. Shayla, may have been desperate to keep you by doing it but I'm not that bitch. I can take care of me and mime. And if I couldn't, I have a family who loves me and would have no problem helping."

"I..."

"I, nothing. I don't wanna hear shit." He blew his breath.

"Let's just find out what he knows and go our separate ways." I opened the door and left him standing there. I walked to the table. Cason and Jason, were in a deep conversation.

"Y'all good?" Cason asked.

"Perfect." I gave him a fake smile.

"Yo boss. I didn't know she was your girl." He looked at me and I turned my head.

"As long as nothing happened, its all good." Pierce sat next to me.

"Now tell me everything." We all sat there listening to him tell us again how it went down with Sway. When he finished, Pierce asked how long he was staying and to let him know once he leaves. Evidently, him and Cason were wondering if they were the target I was supposed to hit as my last job. I couldn't tell them yes or no because Sway always gave me instructions at the last minute.

"Well now that, that's over, I can go home. I'll see you later Cason. Pierce." I hit him with the peace sign and made my way to the car. My chest was bothering me and the limping only slowed me down, from storming off. I turned around to make sure no car was coming. I stepped off the curb to get in my car and was almost thrown on the ground. Pierce grabbed me just in time. A car was so close, if he didn't move me I would've been hit.

"You ok?" He checked me over.

"I'm fine. What was that?"

"Someone tried to run you over. Give me your keys." I handed them to him and he had me move all the way back, as he hit the alarm. Nothing happened so he checked under it and stood up.

"Lets go." He snatched my hand and took me towards his truck.

"She good." Cason was on the phone barking out orders to someone.

"Get in." He helped me in and closed the door. After watching them converse for a few minutes more cars pulled up. I noticed McGuire, Sam, Jeff and a few other guys. As always, McGuire had his computer in his hand and walked around the restaurant and few stores next to it. What was he looking for? A tow truck pulled up and a dude hopped out. I watched one of the other guys go under my car and he was there for a while. I couldn't even tell you when he came up because I fell asleep. Oh well, he'll tell me later.

****

"Rebby. Rebby. Wake up!" I heard and opened my eyes. Tiffany and Kiyah, were standing over me smiling.

"What's wrong?" I looked around and noticed I was at Ingrid's.

"Nothing. We wanna play." They jumped off the bed and ran out the room.

I stood up and ran in the bathroom. The baby was sitting on my bladder and I was hungry. When I finished, I opened the cabinet and grabbed an extra toothbrush, the toothpaste and mouthwash. Ingrid kept extra everything in her house. She always said, anyone could come over and she would always be prepared. As I spit the mouthwash out, I smelled him. The scent he wore was my favorite.

"Do you know how heavy you are with my baby in your stomach?" I rolled my eyes. He stood behind me and rubbed my stomach. I continued brushing my teeth.

"I know this is my baby and I'm sorry for suggesting otherwise." He kissed the side of my neck and his hands went up my shirt.

"Pierceeee." I moaned out quietly. His touch felt very good.

"Yea." He turned me around, sat me on the sink and stood in between my legs.

"Don't ever do no shit like that again." He slid his tongue in my mouth. My hands found the button to his jeans. I opened my legs and moved my panties to the side. I didn't care if my skirt got wet. I needed to feel him inside.

"Reb. We can't." I placed his dick on my clit and let it go up and down.

"Why not." I sucked on his tongue and wrapped one of my arms around his neck. He moved in closer and penetrated me.

"Ahhhhh shit." I yelled out. He covered my mouth with his.

"I'm gonna cum fast Reb, if you don't stop." I was squeezing my muscles around his dick. My clit was throbbing and I wanted him to cum with me.

"I don't care. Fuck me baby." I now had both of my legs wrapped around his waist. My head was leaned back as he sucked on my neck and caressed my chest. I could tell he was about to cum and he knew I was too. He grabbed me tight and both of us moaned out in ecstasy. Neither of us spoke a word. My face was in his neck and I could feel his hands going up and down my back.

"Rebby!" I heard her shouting from downstairs.

"Oh shit." Pierce put his dick away and I hurried to get off the sink. We cleaned ourselves up and by the time Tiffany came in, I was cleaning the sink off with bleach.

"Rebby come play."

"Ok baby. Let me wash my hands and I'll be right down." I kissed her cheek.

"You gonna play with me later?" His dick was on my ass.

"Pierce don't get me started."

"I'm not because when she goes to sleep later, I'ma make up for lost time and for being mean to you."

"Awwww. I love when you're nice to me."

"You better love it now because I won't be nothing nice, when I'm in that pussy."

"How you tryna beat it up and you're supposed to be making up."

"You're lucky, I'm even giving it to you."

"Whatever." And just like that, we were back to our arguing selves.

Ingrid

"Love you bitch but you better had scrubbed my bathroom." I yelled at Rebel when she came down the steps. Pierce was directly behind her with a dumb ass grin on his face.

"Whatever. Pierce wanted to be nasty and he always gets what he wants from me. Sooooo."

"So. You could've take your nasty ass home." I gave her the finger and walked back in the kitchen to check my food.

"How you feeling?" Cason asked and kissed my cheek.

"I'm ok."

"Bae, if you're hurting sit down. My mom, aunt, your mom and even Rebel will help you."

"I don't wanna feel helpless or have people think I'm looking for attention." He made me look at him.

"No one will ever look at you like that. Ingrid, you've gone through a lot and I'm surprised you're even moving around at all."

"Who's gonna take care of the girls? I can't expect anyone to help but you."

"I don't know what that nigga's family did before me but mine is nothing like that." I gave him the side eye.

"Fuck Selina. What I'm saying is, they all love you and waiting for you to ask."

"What if?-"

"Fuck this. I'm calling both of our moms. You need help when I'm not here." I nodded and let him hug me.

My body was slowly healing from the shit Rose did. Not only did she drag me down the street, scrape my body and break my arm. I had to get a few skin grafts on parts of my back because the original skin was completely gone. Then, my arm was broken in two spots. The way she drug me made my forearm snap and my wrist had a crack in it. But listening to her admit how she performed an abortion on me, made me hate her even more. She had no remorse and the look of hate on her face was clear as day.

"Cason, I.-"

"It's done. They'll be here tomorrow." I tried to walk out the kitchen.

"I'm not tryna control you but you're in pain and haven't really relaxed since you came home. Ingrid, I know you're not used to someone loving and taking care of you the correct way but you won't, if you keep tryna stop me."

"I don't want you to think.-"

"I won't think anything. All you need to do is get better and take care of our miracle baby."

"I should've named this one Miracle." He rubbed my belly.

"We can't worry about that, plus this may be my son. We sure can use some more men in this house."

"What you tryna say?" She had her arms across her chest.

"I'm saying three females are gonna drive me crazy." I rolled my eyes.

"Cut it out." I let him lift me up and place me on the island.

"I miss being inside you." His hand was in between my legs, rubbing my clit through my sweats. We hadn't had sex and I tried to go down on him but he wouldn't allow it. He said, it will only make him want me more so he'll wait. Was I worried about him cheating? Absolutely, but I had other shit to worry about at the moment. If I focused on it, I'd accuse him all the time and I didn't wanna push him away.

"Mmmm. I miss you being in there."

"When you ready, let me know." He slid his hands in my sweats. My face was in his neck and I literally was about to cum.

"I'm cumming baby." It felt good as hell.

"And you call me nasty." Rebel said and pushed Cason in the back.

"Ugh, I can be." Cason took his hand out my sweats and placed his fingers in his mouth.

"Damn. I can't wait." I smiled and held on as he helped me down.

"I can't either and I promise to try and be as freaky as before."

"As long as I can feel in that warm pussy, you can lay there." I looked at him.

"Yea, you're right. I need the freaky Ingrid to come out." He walked out and I heard Pierce telling Tiffany and Kiyah, to stop screaming. They always did that when their favorite show comes on.

"She is gonna be beautiful." Rebel had Miracle on her shoulder. I rubbed her hair and kissed her forehead.

"Can you believe, I adopted her and now I'm pregnant?"

"It always happens like that."

"Three kids, though?"

"Hell yea. Girl, you better enjoy these two now because another newborn is gonna take a lot of your attention too."

"I know." I sat next to her and thought about my life. Over the last year, I've gone through abuse, found my true love and dealt with a stalking bitch, who tried to kill me and still wants to. Cason told me not to worry but its always easy for someone to say when they're not the one being hunted. I could say the Sway dude is looking for him but since we're uncertain, I can't be sure.

****

"What do you want Roger?" I was in the store looking for church clothes. This is the first time we were going and none of us had anything to wear.

"Is that my baby?" He pointed to Miracle.

"You know, this isn't your baby because the stupid bitch you cheated on me with killed it." He stood there looking stupid.

"About that? I'm sorry, Ingrid. I had no idea she did that."

"So, why did you ask me if this was your child then? You know, we weren't together after."

"I was hoping she didn't succeed."

"What do you want Roger and I thought you were dead?" My mom told me when the people came to the house, he had passed out from the amount of blood loss. She thought he was dead since no one heard from him. I guess we couldn't be so lucky.

"I miss you." I tossed my head back laughing.

"What do you miss? Whooping my ass, giving me boring sex, cheating on me or allowing a woman to come in and destroy what we were trying to build. I mean there were some serious issues in our relationship and you weren't willing to get help."

"I know and I'm sorry. Can we start over? Let me take you out."

"Now, you of all people know I'm with someone."

"Oh, you mean him." He pulled his phone out and there was a photo with Cason and Odessa hugging. When the hell did this take place?

"How did you get this?"

"Oh, when he stopped by to give his condolences to my sister." I was pissed but I wouldn't show him.

"That was very nice of him."

"So was the kiss they shared." And there was another photo of her reaching up to kiss him.

"Goodbye Roger." I pushed the stroller to leave.

"He's gonna cheat on you just like he did the other chick. Men like him don't change. Look at me. I cheated and you stayed. He knows you're weak and won't leave."

"I'm not weak." I felt my eyes starting to water. I don't know if it's my hormones or the fact, he could still get me this upset.

"Call me, if you want to talk. My number will never change." He kissed me on the cheek and walked off.

I stood there confused as hell. I know he showed me the photos to be smart but how did he get them? The better question is, why did Cason go over to comfort her? It had to be while I was in the hospital, which makes it even worse. I'm in the hospital going through some shit and you're with another bitch. He better have a good ass reason for it. It doesn't even matter because he had no business with her.

Roger

I had to get outta the mall quickly. I didn't want her to

call her man and he come to take

me out. Rose told me a long time ago, that if her brothers had

their minds set on getting someone, nothing anyone said could

stop them. I have to admit Ingrid looked beautiful but I could

still see the weakness in her face and hear it in her voice. She

may have become tougher when it came to me but that

insecure chick, will always be there. I have no idea why I

asked if that was my kid, after hearing the shit Rose told her.

The day I was shot, Rose told me she was going to kill

Ingrid because she was over her getting in the middle of our

shit. No idea what she was speaking of when we both knew

Cason had her on lock. Anyway, I followed her to and knew

shit would go bad, when I noticed Ingrid's car out there. I

hopped out and attempted to stop her from going to the door

but once she pulled the gun out, I backed away.

Rose knocked on the door, punched Mrs. Lopez in the face and pulled the gun out on her father. She made me tie them up and then went straight for Ingrid. I barged in the room and heard her telling Cason she was at my parents' house, which is untrue. A few seconds later, my phone rang and it was my sister asking where I was. The family came to the house and were looking for me. She had me tell my sister to say, I was at some cemetery. Long story short, she sent Cason on a wild goose chase to make sure she'd have enough time to deal with Ingrid.

She tried to get me to rape her but I wasn't having that shit. Unfortunately, she shot me in the arm and I fell on the ground. I've never in my life ben shot and a nigga was in extreme pain. I laid there listening to her replay all the things she did to Ingrid and was sickened at how crazy the bitch really was. I blamed myself because had I not cheated, we wouldn't be in this situation. After revealing it, she pointed her gun and I saw Ingrid's eyes and turned my head. I yelled for help and Rose started shooting and took her hostage. I couldn't believe the lengths she was going through to have me.

The ambulance came, took me in and I had a shattered collarbone but it wasn't anything too bad. I swear, the entire time in the hospital, I just knew Cason would come get me. When I opened my eyes and no one was in the room, I knew he probably had no idea where I was. I contacted my mom, she came to get me and I've been at her house ever since, which is how I captured the photo of my sister and Cason.

Supposedly, he came to comfort her but I'm sure it was to see if I were there. It didn't matter to me because the look of shock on Ingrid's face, told me she had no clue. Not only that, my father's funeral took place at the same time she was in the hospital. She had to be feeling some kind of way about it. Shit, anyone would.

I found out about her through Rose, who called and told me where she was. The dumb bitch had been staying with her mom. She claimed her mom would never give her up and invited me over. At first, I told her no, if her mom was home. After hearing about her aunt, I didn't need her mom seeing my face and putting two and two together. However; she contacted me today and asked for me to come. Her mom was working a double and wouldn't be home until tomorrow.

"Open the door." I spoke in the phone from my car. I parked down the street in case her mom came home for lunch or something.

"Hey." I smiled staring at her belly. I wanted Ingrid to be my kids mother but things changed.

"Roger." I moved past and waited for her to lock the door.

"Why Rose? Was it that serious?" I questioned her about doing that fake abortion shit.

"To me, it was. You kept fucking me and pushed me to the side for her. She was always in the way."

"She was my woman. I would've still taken care of my child with you." She sucked her teeth.

"I told you to terminate it but when you said no, what could I do?" She didn't say a word.

"Instead, you took her chance of having kids away from her."

"She didn't deserve your kids. I DID!" I saw this shit escalating and being she's crazy, I had to do something to calm her down.

"Do you need anything for the baby?" And just like that, I saw her relaxing.

"Yes. Come see." She grabbed my hand and had me follow her up the steps.

"We're having a boy." My smile became wider, hearing her say that. The room was all blue, with a rocking chair, crib and anything possible for a newborn. I noticed an envelope on the changing table and opened it.

"What are these?"

"Those are bonds for the baby."

"It's over two million dollars in them." Shit, I had money in my bank account but not a million dollars and she has two, plus some.

"I worked a lot Roger and saved my money. I always knew, I'd have kids and wanted to make sure they'd be set, if anything happened to me." I saw her eyes becoming glassy.

"What's wrong?" I sat her on my lap.

60

"Cason's gonna kill me."

"You don't know that. He's like your brother. I'm sure if you talked to him and apologized." She got up off my lap without letting me finish.

"He's already been here and told my mom, who by the way said she understood." My eyes grew wide.

"What?"

"I know right. She didn't rat me out about being here but she told him, if he finds me to make sure she can have a proper burial for me."

"Damn. Well, you can come stay at my mom's. That's where I've been and I'm sure he won't come there."

"I don't trust your sister." Now I was confused because they were hanging out before all of this other shit went down.

"Why?"

"She's been posting stuff on social media about her and Cason."

"What's up with them?"

"I don't know but there's a photo of them hugging and her about to kiss him. I'm not sure if he knows yet, but I can

61

guarantee, he'll go over there. How the hell did she even get that?"

"I took it and gave it to her." I explained and she was laughing.

"Good. I hope that bitch see's it and leaves him. I know she's the reason he wants to kill me. Maybe if she wasn't in his life, he'd give me a pass." Now, I know she's crazy. He may have forgiven her for the shit at the Christmas party but pulling a gun out and almost killing her; I don't see him giving her a second chance, at all.

****

After I left from seeing Rose, I went to my mothers. I drove around the back and parked in the garage. I never knew if he had someone watching and the way our house is, there's a separate entrance that you only know about, if someone told you.

I heard my mother and sister in there talking about getting Cason. I couldn't believe my mom was entertaining the shit. This is the exact reason my father was dead now. The two of them scheming and him trying to stop it. I walked past and went upstairs. A few minutes later, there was a knock at my door.

"What?" I flipped my television on and put my back against the headboard.

"Is that anyway to speak to the woman who's gonna help you get Ingrid back?" She stood in front of me smirking.

"And how the hell are you gonna do that?" She passed me her phone and unless she had another person's number logged in under Cason's name, the text messages were pretty heavy. My sister was sending explicit ass messages and even though he didn't incriminate himself too much, he definitely entertained her.

"These are just messages."

"Yup. Messages that says he'll be stopping by later to get some head." I looked back at the message and sure shit, she offered to top him off and he agreed.

"You sure about this? I don't see this going the same way you do."

"Positive."

"And how is that?" She sat on my bed.

63

"Well, from what I hear, Ingrid has been out the hospital for a minute now but they haven't had sex."

"How the hell do you know that?"

"Selina overheard him telling her cousin." I didn't even know she spoke to her. Rose had to tell her.

"What does that have to do with you?"

"Duhhhh. It means a man in need of sexual favors will do anything to release. And you bet I'ma let him fuck me anyway he wants." She stood up and headed to the door.

"Oh. I need you to be gone by seven. He'll be here at eight and in case he wants to roam the house, I don't want him to see you." She winked and walked out. I hope she had faith in this suicide mission because I damn sure didn't. I see this going wrong in so many ways but at least she told me so I could get far away.

Cason

"What's up Ingrid?" I asked. Her and Miracle came from the mall not too long ago and she hasn't said two words to me. I've been asking her shit and she'd just ignore me.

"INGRID!" I saw her jump and roll her eyes.

"Why are you here Cason?"

"What the fuck you mean? I live here."

"No. You live in that condo, you don't wanna get rid of. Is that where you fuck your ho's."

"My ho's? I don't have anyone else." She stood up and tried to walk away.

"Cason, I love you but I won't allow you to stress me out with your bullshit lies."

"Say what the fuck you mean."

"Where were you when I was in the hospital?"

"I was with you."

"I mean, when you left. Where were you?" I stood there staring at her eyes getting glassy. I had two choices. One... I could be truthful and tell her I went to see Odessa, in hopes of running into Roger. Or two… pretend not to know what she's talking about. If she's becoming this upset, I'm sure someone told her something but what? I went with option three, which is start an argument, leave and try to figure out how much she knows and who told her.

"I don't know what happened from the time you left the house until you came back but this fucked up attitude ain't shit, I'm tryna deal with."

"Ok." She shook her head and walked to the door.

"Get the fuck out."

"What?"

"You heard me. Get the fuck out." She opened the door and leaned her head on it.

"I thought you would tell me the truth. I was willing to hear you out and try to understand why? But this fucked up way you're going about the situation, is funny to me." She wiped the tears falling.

"You've never lied to me as far as I know and this arrogant, ignorant man standing here only proves, you are in fact hiding something. I just hope, its worth all this." She pointed to herself and left me standing there. I ran my hand over my face and closed the door. I had no business leaving the house to see this bitch.

When Ingrid was in the hospital, Odessa hit me up thinking we were cool because I stopped by when her pops died. I only did it because I was tryna catch her brother there. Anyway, she thanked me and somehow, we ended up discussing other things, that led into explicit ass text messages. Now being my girl wasn't ready for sex, like any man, I entertained them but never said much. They were more on the lines of let me just sick your dick, come play in my pussy and her visualizing me being inside her. I told her, I'd stop by to let her suck me off but the real reason is to search the house for her brother.

Roger hadn't been to his place in a long time and the only other place he may go besides his mom's, is Rose and she isn't home either. I figured because she wanted me so bad she'd allow me full access to the house. When a bitch is desperate they'd do anything to get a man over, which is what

Odessa did. I tried to call Ingrid again on my way over and she kept sending me to voicemail. I parked in the driveway and noticed it was after nine. I wonder if he'd be here, thinking I wasn't coming. I started to knock on the door and she opened it, in a small ass robe.

"What up?" I moved past her and went in the living room. I heard her suck her teeth. Don't ask me why, when she knew how I felt about her tryna be sexy. Plus, I was here for one reason.

"Lets take this to your room. I know you have one here." I walked up the steps behind her and shook my head. She had no panties on and made sure to pretend something fell. Her pussy was wide open. Once she opened the bedroom door, she excused herself and went in the bathroom.

I left and looked in the two rooms next to hers. I ran to the closets and checked under the bed. One of the rooms was bare but I had a feeling it's the one, her brother was staying at. I checked the hall closet and went back down the steps. I checked the kitchen closet and was about to try the basement. I heard her yelling my name and opened the refrigerator. I pretended to be thirsty and grabbed a water.

"I would've gotten you something to drink." Odessa was now full blown naked.

"I'm good."

"Cason, why are you acting nervous?" She pushed me against the counter.

"Why you acting desperate? You got me here, which means I'm yours."

"Oh, your mine for the night. Come on." She grabbed my hand and took me in the living room.

"Cason, I've missed this." She sat on my lap and started grinding her body on mine. My man started waking up.

"Odessa, I don't think.- She hopped off and unbuttoned my jeans.

"You don't think what?" I was now fighting her hands to make her stop.

"I have a girl and got dammit." She pulled my boxers down and her mouth felt so damn good on my dick. I heard a light knock at the front door and the bitch didn't move. Me; on the other hand, wasn't tryna cheat or get caught slipping.

"You know, I'm not gonna tell. Let me give you what I know you need." I heard the knocking get louder.

"Shit, Odessa. Get up." I tried lifting her head but she was sucking the hell outta my dick.

BANG! BANG!

"Shit, get the door."

"Ughhhhh." She was aggravated and answered the door only showing her head. I hurried and placed my dick in my jeans and thanked God for stepping in. The only problem was, he helped me in one way but shitted on me in another.

"Why the hell are you answering the door naked and where's Cason?" I heard Ingrid, clear as day.

"Because I was about to finish sucking his dick and then let him fuck me silly. Rose was right about you always being in the way." I saw Odessa's head go back when my girl punched her.

"Ingrid, let me explain."

70

"Explain what Cason? Why you over here getting your dick sucked by a chick, who's not your woman?" She moved closer to me.

"I asked, if I could go down on you and you said no because you'd wanna be inside me after. I guess this is why she's naked and your dick is still hard. You were gonna fuck her too." I looked down and it wasn't brick but enough to know.

"You are a fucking piece of shit." I grabbed her arm.

"It took me a long time to get pregnant and the doctor said no stress, right. You of all people should've been the last person to put me in a position to lose a child. If you wanted to be single, you should've said it. I would've been hurt and fought for you but if its what you really wanted, I would've let you go."

"I'm.-"

"No, you're not. You know, I'd rather hear about it, then seeing this." She pointed to the bitch who was still naked.

"Why would you think he'd be faithful?" She snapped her neck at Odessa.

"You're right. How can a man be faithful when there's nothing but a shitload of ho's out there? Ho's, looking for a come up and a stupid ass nigga falling right into their trap?"

"I'll be a ho. I'll be that same ho to keep him satisfied. The same one, he's been texting and seeing for the last few weeks." I swore Ingrid's head was gonna fall off by how hard she turned.

"You've been texting and seeing her?"

"Not the way she's making it seem." She folded her arms.

"Cason, no need to cover up. Shit, you caught now." She passed Ingrid her phone and came over to me. This bitch had the nerve to hug me from behind like she was my girl.

"This has been going on since I was in the hospital. Are?-" She stopped speaking and the phone fell outta Ingrid's hand. I was literally fighting with Odessa, who had her hands in my jeans. Her facial expression spoke volumes.

"Yo, back the fuck up." I tossed her on the couch.

"You can have him." I watched her storm out the house and ran behind her.

72

POW! POW! I heard and ducked. Ingrid had a gun pointed at me.

"Stay the fuck away from me."

"Did you just shoot at me?" She let another shot off and grazed my ear. I could feel a little blood trickling. I had no idea she was familiar with a gun. When the hell did she take shooting lessons?

"I swear if you come closer, I won't miss." She screamed out with tears rushing down her face.

"Ingrid." I took a step and she let off a shot, barely missing my face. She opened the car door, sat down, gave me one disgusting look and pulled off. I ran in the house to grab my things and Odessa was playing with herself on the couch. I was not about to indulge in anything with her. It would really kill any chance I may have in getting Ingrid back. I could look at it as I'm not cheating but then again, its still fucked up on all levels.

"Don't hit my line no more." I told her and walked out. I blocked her ass the moment I got to the car. I never should've brought my ass here and found Roger another way.

73

****

"Oh my God! What happened to you? PIERCE!" Rebel screamed when she saw me. My ear was still bleeding and I had blood all over my shirt.

"What the fuck you yelling for?" He came downstairs looking like he just woke up.

"Something happened to Cason." She came in with some paper towels.

"What happened to you? Who did this?" I looked at Rebel and she had a confused look on her face.

"Ingrid."

"She caught you?" He sat on the couch.

"Yup."

"Caught you what?" Rebel had her hands on her hips.

"I told your ass not to go." I hated for someone to say, I told you so.

"What did she catch you doing? Never mind, I'll call her." She left us and I explained what happened.

"Damn. For all that, you should've went ahead and fucked her, or at least let her finish sucking your dick."

74

POP! Rebel smacked him on the back of his head.

"Bi.-" He was about to call her out.

"Huh? What you say Pierce?"

"Don't hit me again." She mushed him in the head.

"Alright. Don't say shit when.-" She waved him off.

"Ingrid isn't answering her phone. What did you do?"

"You may as well tell her because she's gonna try and fuck it outta me and if she do, I'm straight telling." I busted out laughing,

I started telling her what the motive was and how shit ended up bad. She was shaking her head and even threw the remote at me. Her and Ingrid, were some violent ass females. I asked for some a towel and she told me to kiss her ass. I should've never out myself in the position to be with another woman. I couldn't debate anything she said but isn't that the pot calling the kettle black. When I said that, she damn near went into labor the way she cursed me out and tried to hit me. Pierce thought all of it was funny.

"I'm out. Your chick is crazy and I had enough crazy for the night."

"I hope she makes you suffer forever." I turned around.

"I'll allow her to let me suffer for a little while but Ingrid ain't going nowhere."

"Don't underestimate her."

"Nah shorty. Don't underestimate me." I walked over to her.

"I fucked up, so I'ma deal with being alone but trust me when I say, she ain't going nowhere."

"How you gonna try and.-"

"Because she's my fucking woman and no other nigga will ever bed her." I went to leave.

"Oh, and you can tell her when she finally calls. That if I find out she gives Roger, another five minutes of her time and not tell me, I'll kill her." The look on Rebel's face told me she knew I wasn't playing.

I never told Ingrid someone called and told me she was with Roger at the mall. When she came home and didn't speak, I knew he said something and figured it pissed her off. Now, I'm starting to think he's the one who had her upset about things I did. Of course, I still didn't know what she knew, but anything to have her as upset as she was, is enough to know his

ass is up to no good. I got something for his ass though. He

wasn't at the house but I'm sure he's staying there. It may take

me a little longer to get him but I will.

Rose

"Bitchhhhhhh. I know you lying." I was cracking up as Odessa filled me in on what went down at her house.

"Girl. The bitch was about to cry."

"I'm so fucking happy somebody bust her bubble."

"Shit, I thought he was gonna kill her when she shot at him."

"WHATTTTTT?"

"Hell yea, bitch. He tried to run after her and she shot his ass. She started yelling for him to stay away and the next one wouldn't miss."

"Are you sure she shot him? I don't see him allowing her to live afterwards."

"I saw blood coming down his ear when he came in but I can't be sure."

"Wow!"

"Shit! I'd shoot a bitch over that good ass dick."

"I do not wanna hear about Cason's dick."

"I'm just saying."

"Anyway, let me go. My mom, just walked in."

"Hey ma." I walked down the steps and stopped when I noticed Cason standing there.

"What's going on?"

"Get dressed." He said it calmly.

"What's wrong with your ear?" Maybe what Odessa said, is true.

"I'm not gonna tell you again to get dressed."

"Ma, what's going on?" My heart was racing.

"I told you to leave that woman alone." I didn't get to respond because Cason snatched me up. I almost fell up the steps because he had my shirt.

"Why are you doing this?" He ignored me and tapped away at his phone. I stood there staring at him and realized how sexy he was.

"Cason, do you ever think about what we could've been? I've always been attracted to you." I put my hand on his chest and he punched me in the face. I must've passed out

79

because I woke up with my sneakers on. My mom stood over me shaking her head and I didn't see him anywhere.

"Hurry up."

"Ma, what's going on?" This time she grabbed me by the hair and basically dragged me down the steps. Did no one care about me being pregnant?

"Why are you grabbing my hair?" She never responded and the two of us walked to a truck. I got in and she followed.

The entire ride to wherever we were going, her and Cason spoke about nonsense. Neither of them answered when I tried to talk and when they decided to eat, I wasn't offered any food. My mother said, where I was going, I shouldn't have food on my stomach. I sat in the back starving and wondering where they were taken me.

After about an hour, the truck stopped in front of a huge looking house. I thought my eyes were deceiving me when MJ, Pierce, Alex and a few others came out. If his cousins were here, this couldn't be good. I glanced at my mom and saw tears falling down her face. I'm pissed no one is telling me anything.

Cason stepped out and my door opened. He yanked me out and damn near drug me to the front. All of the guys shook their heads at me. We walked in and upstairs a flight of steps. It looked like a medical facility but I've never been here so I couldn't be sure. He pushed me in a room and told me to put a gown on. I was about to ask why but the door closed.

"Let's go." I heard when it reopened and it was my mom. She still had a sad look on her face.

"I can't believe you got me caught up in your bullshit."

"Huh?" She led me in a room and left me there with Cason, two ladies who appeared to be nurses and a doctor.

"This is what's gonna happen." He pushed me by the table.

"The doctor is about to give you a C-section and take the baby out."

"WHATTTTT?" I started panicking. His hands were now around my throat and I could barely breathe.

"Like I was saying. He's gonna take the baby out your stomach and then I'm gonna kill you. Are we clear?" I let the tears fall.

"Are we clear?" I nodded the best I could and he let go. My body hit the floor but not that hard.

"Cason, I'm sorry."

"Get on the table."

"Cason please. I don't want my baby to grow up without a mother."

"GET ON THE FUCKING TABLE!" I jumped and stood up.

"You got one time to try and run and you and that baby, will die."

"But.-"

"But nothing. You're lucky I'm allowing this baby to live, even though you took my girls. Then you invite the nigga over to my parents' house for a Christmas party and he almost gets her. You pull a gun out on her there and again at her parents' house; after you revealed the bullshit you did to her. And let's not forget the hospital and court shit. Did you really think I'd let you roam freely?"

"Cason, we've been friends for a very long time."

"Exactly! Which is why I knocked your stupid ass out for even tryna attempt to fuck me, to save your life."

"Rose what type of shit you on?" Pierce yelled out by the door.

"Cason don't do this."

"You did this." He pointed to the table.

"If I say it again, your body will hit the floor." I didn't say a word and hopped on the table.

I felt the two women grab my arms, strap them down and then my legs. The doctor placed monitors on my stomach and chest. When they finished everything, I asked to speak to my mother. She came in with that same sad look.

"Why couldn't you leave that woman alone?"

"I loved him and.-" She smacked me across the face.

"You risked everything for a man, who's not even here to save you. He's still going to be alive, while you're dead. Here. Sign this." She placed a pen in my hand and since I'm sure it was custody papers, I signed the best I could. With me dead and Roger is next, my mother is the only one I trusted.

"I love you Rose. I'll take good care of the baby." She stepped out and I saw Cason give the doctor an ok, to start.

"Am I gonna get anesthesia?"

"For what? You're gonna feel exactly what my girl did."

The doctor stood at the bottom of my body and I felt the knife cut into my stomach. I screamed out and yet; no one cared. One of the nurses placed a pair of earphones on the doctor, I guess so he could concentrate. Every time he made a new cut, I felt it.

"Bring me the forceps." I could hear everything going on and at this point, I had no cry left. My child was being removed from my stomach and Cason was waiting to kill me. Why didn't I leave Ingrid alone? Was Roger worth all of this? I heard my child cry and saw the gun pointed at my forehead. I tried to say a prayer in hopes to make it to Heaven but he gave me no time.

"What you gonna do?" I asked Ingrid. We were at my place with the girls.

"Odessa went outta her way to make sure I knew everything. In my eyes, he wanted to be single and found out. Otherwise; why would he allow her to tell me." She shrugged her shoulders.

"Do you really believe that?"

"To be honest, I don't know what to believe anymore. Each time I feel like the two of us are in a good place, he messes up." I nodded because it did seem like that.

"I'm serious. When Pierce was shot and he called me by her name, I was hurt until he explained why he did it. Then, this nonsense happens and we're right back at not speaking or seeing one another. And before yo ask, of course, I miss him and would love to be under him but all I'm doing is repeating the cycle."

"What cycle?"

"Roger had me in the same situation and the only difference is, he got high and hit me. Its like, I'm the perfect woman for men, yet; they can't keep their dick to themselves. Is my sex game whack or maybe they wanna be with women who are more experienced than me? Who knows? I do know, I'm tired of trying to figure it out."

"I understand and I'd probably feel; no I would feel the same but he's not gonna let you go."

"The crazy part about what you told me he said, is I believe him. Its one way to make him stay away, and after I deliver, I'm going to do it."

"What's that?"

"Fuck someone else." She said it like he'd let her.

"Ok, so you want to make these kids motherless."

"Bitch, really?"

"I'm serious. He messed up and if you don't wanna be with him, that's one thing but his exact words to me were, *"She's my woman and no other nigga will bed her."* In my mind, that means you and the nigga will die." I stood up to get Kiyah off the chair she was standing on.

"Oh, so its ok for him to bed other bitches?"

"Hell no. Unfortunately, you went from one crazy nigga to another. You picked him." I walked Kiyah in the other room and Tiffany was jumping all over the couch.

"Its time for a damn nap." Ingrid agreed. I looked at the clock and it was 11:30. Ingrid finished feeding Miracle and the two of us fed the girls and put them to sleep.

I definitely slept for a long time because I woke up and Ingrid was gone. Pierce was sitting next to me eating chicken, mashed potatoes and macaroni and cheese. Tiffany had her own food in the highchair. You damn right I grabbed a piece of his plate and he popped my hand.

"Reb, yours is in the kitchen. Why you eating off me?"

"Because you make yours taste better than mine for some reason."

"No. You lazy as hell and instead of asking, you dipping in my shit."

"Well, you dip in my shit almost every night and I don't pop you." He shook his head smirking.

"You damn right." He licked his fingers and went in the kitchen to grab mine. I sure did eat my food and his too.

****

"Babe, I'll be right back. I need the bathroom." Pierce and I, were at the movie theatre watching something he picked out.

"Bring me back some sour patch kids." I put my hand out.

"Man, you got money."

"I want your money."

"You riding my dick in here when you get back?" I looked around and was happy we were at an early showing. It was maybe three other people here and his ass was not quiet.

"Hell no."

"Then pay for my shit."

"What does that have to do with anything."

"You want me to pay for something so the way I see it is, you need to compensate me."

"But its your candy."

"Candy you'll stick your hand in to eat too." I sucked my teeth and walked off.

I finished in the bathroom and walked up to the food section. I was like a kid in the candy store, picking out different ones with the cashier.

"Hey sexy." I didn't even turn around. His voice still sent chills down my spine but he was someone, I haven't spoken to in years and I had no problem keeping it that way.

"Is that all miss?"

"Yes. Thank you." I tried to back up and felt him.

"Move!"

"Damn, I didn't know you were pregnant." He licked his lips.

"Don't you have a woman? Why are you bothering me?" He wouldn't let me move past him.

"Daddy, did the movie start?" Some little boy came over. He was a spitting image of my ex, which only made the memories of that night, resurface.

"Not yet. Can you give me a minute to talk to my friend?"

"Hello." He spoke and asked his dad for money to play the video games.

"Where you been Rebel?"

"Away from you." He still refused to let me move away.

"I'm so sorry for hurting you. I miss you." He went to hug me and the bullshit started.

"SYEED! Are you fucking serious right now?" I looked and Selina came towards him and her stomach was poking out.

"Selina, what the fuck you yelling for?"

"I know you're not trying to fuck this whore." Syeed gave me a crazy look.

"What is she talking about Rebel?"

"Its doesn't matter. She's a hater and always has been. Have fun with my leftovers." This time I walked by and what she screamed out, embarrassed the shit outta me.

"Your leftovers? Ha! Bitch, remember you caught him with me. I fucked him first which means you had my leftovers. Stupid bitch."

I couldn't even argue with her because what she said was true. We may have been a couple but the fact she had him first, makes him, her leftovers. This is the exact reason I didn't wanna have sex with him in the first place. Granted, I had no idea he was bedding someone else but my motto was always wait until we're married. Unfortunately, I wanted to please him and all it did was cause me more pain. Now she bragging and I'm pregnant so guess who can't beat her ass?

"Selina, why you look pissed off?" Pierce said and snatched the candy out my hand. I hate, he was being ignorant at the moment.

"What up Sy?" I had no idea they knew one another.

"Your fake ass baby momma tried to fuck him."

"Selina! What the fuck is wrong with you?" Syeed shouted.

"She was all in your face when I came out the bathroom. Ho's are known to do that when they trying to fuck. Isn't that right, ho?"

"Yo, Selina. Don't make me knock you the fuck out and what she talking about Reb?" I looked at Syeed and my hatred for him grew. Why did he have to cheat? He brought this drama to me.

"I wanna go home."

"Ok. But I need to know what's up?"

"Pierce, please take me home."

"Yea, cuz. Take the fucking whore home. Don't you have some tricks to call?" Pierce yanked Selina up by the hair and Syeed stood there. I guess he knew not to fuck with him.

"I told you before, not to disrespect her and you're showing your ass. Get the fuck on, yo." He pushed her back but not hard. I would've done way more.

"Really, Pierce!" She got in his face.

"You know, ever since you and Cason met these bitches, its been nothing but bullshit. Their destroying our family and both of you are allowing it. I've stayed quiet but the truth is, this is the bitch who Syeed cheated on me with. The one, who tried to fight me when I was pregnant with Syeed Jr. And the one, who Syeed can't seem to let go of." I covered my mouth when she said that. I would never admit that to anyone.

"Nah, he cheated on her with you."

"I slept with him first."

"And you're bragging about it. You sound dumb as hell Selina. Standing here admitting he still has feelings for her and that she caught you fucking him. You need to take your ass home."

"Don't tell me what the fuck to do." I saw her son coming towards us.

"Pierce, calm down. Her son is coming and.-"

"Bitch, don't worry about my son." I turned my head and the bitch snuck me. I didn't wanna fight in front of her son, or the fact I'm pregnant but she caused this. I started raining blows on her. Somehow, she tripped me and I fell on my back and hit my head against the wall. That's literally all I remember.

Pierce

"Hey! You good!" I asked Rebel. After falling at the movies, I brought her straight to the hospital. I wasn't taking any chances on her losing my kid.

"Pierce, let me explain."

"I don't give a fuck about what he did to you in the past. No, I don't like it but it's your past. Ima get in Selina's ass though." I moved closer to her.

"Reb, on some real shit. You are the best thing that's happened to me; well besides me finding out about Tiffany. Selina said some foul shit but I don't think that way at all. Your past, is your past and as long as you don't do no more jobs with him or any other niggas, we good."

"I already told him, I wasn't."

"Everyone in a person's family won't always love the person you choose. And I know the reason she don't care for you, is over a nigga. A nigga who did you dirty and she's mad because he still loved you."

"Pierce, I don't want him and when she called me all those whores.-" I wiped her eyes.

"Jealousy is her biggest downfall."

"Huh?"

"Selina has been a jealous girl all her life. It has nothing to do with you and more of herself." I sat down.

"She was in love with a man who had a woman. Unfortunately, she didn't know right away but she definitely was aware when you walked in on them."

"That's crazy."

"It is. See, we knew she was messing with someone but evidently, he told her he was in a relationship. Long story short, Selina hid the pregnancy which is why none of us knew; including him. We made her tell the guy and he came by to meet the family. He explained about his girl and not being ready for a kid but he would step up and handle his responsibilities. I don't know how they ended up in the bed but she told us a month later, they were a couple."

"That's because I left him."

"Try not to let her bother you."

"Pierce, I'm not tryna bring drama in your family. Ingrid and I, only wanna love y'all but it's so much and.-"

"And I don't care if she likes you or not. You're gonna be in my family for a very long time." I pulled the ring out my pocket. Her hands were covering her mouth.

"Rebel, I know we bump heads a lot but I fucking love the shit outta you. You're a great stepmother to my daughter and I don't wanna lose you to no bullshit." She now had tears coming down her face.

"Are you gonna say yes or not?"

"You just couldn't keep the momentum, could you?" She put her hand out and let me slide the big ass rock on. Hell yea, I picked out a humongous ring. Her ass ain't getting another one so she better cherish this one.

"Whatever. You lucky I asked. I was gonna sit it on the bed at home and wait for you to call me."

"Ughhhh."

"What?"

"Nothing. Come here." She wrapped her arms around my neck and kissed me.

"You know my dick hard, right?" I pointed and she smirked.

"Maybe I should handle my fiancé." I went to close the door and my mom walked in with Tiffany, Kiyah and my aunt. *Guess, that ain't happening.* Rebel waved and they saw the ring.

"OH MY GOD! He finally asked." My mom was more excited than Rebel.

"I'm so happy you'll be part of the family. Now if we can get Cason and Ingrid on the right track." My aunt said and sat down.

"That's not gonna happen anytime soon." Ingrid walked in with Miracle. My aunt took her right out her arms. All of us sucked our teeth. She could be mad right now but we all know, neither of them are going anywhere.

****

"Yo, What the fuck Selina?" I slammed the door to her house. Syeed was sitting on the couch shaking his head. Its not that he's scared of us but he learned a long time ago to stay outta family business. He knew exactly the type of person Selina is.

"Goodbye Pierce." She tried to walk away.

"What the hell is wrong with you? Huh? You that threatened by her, that you'll swing while she's pregnant?"

"So am I?"

"Exactly! Which is the exact reason you had no fucking business putting your hands on her."

"I told her that shit and got in her ass too." Syeed said and Selina sucked her teeth.

"What do you want Selina? I mean, you don't care for Ingrid and she doesn't want him or even did anything for you to turn on her. Rebel hasn't seen or been around this nigga in years and yet; you're attacking her. She can't control his feelings. And if you knew he still felt something for her, why your dumb ass still with him?" She couldn't say anything.

"Look Selina." I lifted her face.

"You don't have to like her and I'd never ask you too but she's about to be my wife so I suggest you get comfortable seeing her at family functions."

"WHAT?"

"You heard me."

"How the hell you marrying her? Y'all haven't been together that long."

"I don't care if I met her two months ago. If I wanna marry her, I will." I made my way to the door because I couldn't listen to her stupidity any longer.

"Syeed is no threat to me as you can see. We still cool, even though I know he may have some feelings left for my girl. However, her feelings aren't reciprocated, therefore; there's no worry."

"That's what you think."

"You can throw shade all you want but we all know, she doesn't want him. You need to be confident in your spot, otherwise; he's gonna bounce." She glanced over at him.

"Selina, if I had any chance with Rebel back in the day to make her take me back after cheating, it went out the window when she saw your stomach and I admitted to getting you pregnant. Of course, I still love her. She was my first love but I would never step on his toes or even put you in a position

99

to feel challenged." I stood there listening to him break it down for her.

"Selina when she broke up with me, I knew we could never be together. It took me a while to get over her but I swear since you've been in my life, I haven't even thought about another woman. Did I cheat to get you? Yes. But I learned my lesson and seeing Rebel hurting and crying over what I did, made me realize, I'd never make another woman go through that; especially my kids' mother." He wiped the tears streaming down her face.

"I am in love with you Selina but Pierce is right. If you don't get this jealousy shit under control, I will leave you." He stood up and left her sitting there.

"I'm scared Pierce." I walked back over to her.

"Of what?"

"Him doing the same thing. I knew he had a woman and still slept with him, just to see if I could get him. When I realized he wouldn't leave her, I left him alone."

"So why did you sleep with him again?"

"I don't even know. We went to tell his family about the baby and he took me in his room, to show me he was looking for a job on the computer. I started kissing him and he tried to stop me but I kept going. Next thing I know, we're having sex and she walks in."

"Selina you were foul as fuck and if he did cheat on you, it would be exactly what you deserve. Lucky for you, he claims to have never cheated and he must be telling the truth because you didn't debate it."

"I don't think he did." She wiped her eyes and laid back on the couch.

"Ok, so don't make him."

"What?" She sat up.

"A man doesn't want a nagging bitch all the time. He don't want you accusing him each time he leaves the house or stalking his phone. If you trust him, then trust me. Selina, Rebel is not your enemy and neither is Ingrid. Stop taking your anger out on them."

"Whatever. The bi.-" She caught herself.

"She hit me while I was pregnant."

"Oh, so you're gonna skip the fact you swung first?" She waved me off.

"She's gonna wanna fight you after she drops the load." I shrugged my shoulders and stood up. She looked at me.

"Don't look at me like that. If you weren't my cousin, I would've slid your ass myself." I opened the door.

"I can't wait to see that fight."

"Petty."

"I'm serious. Both of y'all were throwing jabs. I'll make sure to have popcorn." I hit her with the peace sign and closed the door.

I was serious about my fiancé wanting to fight her. Rebel, is not about to let that shit go and I'm not gonna ask her too. Selina, has to deal with whatever consequences come her way for the bullshit she pulled.

Ingrid

"Why are you calling my phone Roger?" I was changing Miracle's diaper.

Ever since I caught Cason red handed with Odessa, I haven't seen him nor did I want to. I'd drop the kids off to his mom when I knew he was at Pierce's house and pick them up, once he left. A few times his mom brought them to me. I'm sure Cason could make it his business to come here but he was definitely giving me time to cool off about the cheating shit, from what his mom told me. I don't know why he told her that. I'm over it and moved on. He's not about to make me lose this baby with his infidelities or any other stress.

"I heard what happened with my sister and your man."

"I'm sure you did since you're the one who called and told me, he was there."

The night I caught Cason, its because Roger called me. I tried to disguise the hurt when he described my man's car after I accused him of lying. He hung the phone up and sent me a photo instead and to say I was hurt, would be underestimating it. To know he saw her while I was in the hospital and then left to see her after an argument was like a stab in my heart. I left one crazy cheater, only to end up with another one.

I'm pretty sure Odessa had the shit set up, which is exactly why she answered naked. You can't imagine how broken my heart was seeing him fixing his clothes. Then, to hear her mention the texts and phone calls only intensified my hatred for him. How could he do me the same way Roger did? I swear men tell women anything to keep them around, knowing the whole time its too hard to stay faithful. I don't even wanna think what would've happened if I didn't show up or what did when I left. All it would do is drive me crazy and I needed my sanity for the girls.

Cason's tried to call me over the last two weeks and each time, I ignored him. I left his messages unread and the flowers he sent to my job, I had returned. There was nothing he could say to me right now and you would think, Roger would get the point to but no. His ass is on the phone pleading his case about not knowing the entire story of what took place in the house. He may not have been there but Odessa had a big mouth and probably couldn't wait to tell him.

"I miss you Ingrid." I took the phone away from my ear and looked at it. Did he really say that?

"I'm serious. Do you think we can try again? I promise not to lay hands on you, cheat or do drugs."

"Roger." I lifted Miracle up and got her ready to go. Cason's mom was on her way to get them for church. Today everyone was going but she wanted to go early for some reason.

"At least, let me see you." I heard a knock at the door and made my way down the steps.

"Please."

"I'll think about it." I hung up and tried my hardest not to stare at how good Cason looked. His mom must've asked him to pick them up.

He had on a navy-blue suit with gold cufflinks on the wrist. His shoes were shiny as hell and I could see his dreads were freshly done. The one thing, I wanted to see was covered by his pants. My body was feenin for him and he knew it. He cleared his throat and it made me look up. I handed him Miracle and called Kiyah. She was in the other room watching television. She came over with her puffy dress and shiny shoes. Her hair was done and she had a little purse to match.

"Here." I gave her five dollars to put in it for the offering. Its Sunday and you know that collection plate will go around, at least twice.

"I'll see you in a few." I kissed her cheek and did the same with Miracle.

"Do I get one?" I shut the door and leaned on it. I ran upstairs and looked out the window to see him placing girls in the car seat. I went in my drawer, pushed some clothes to the side, grabbed my toy and went to work thinking about Cason. I was sleepy afterwards and almost didn't go.

I threw on the mid length peach dress, I purchased to match the girls. Once I finished getting dressed, I grabbed all three of us, some extra clothes to take to their grandmothers. As always, she was having a big dinner and she said, we better show up. I checked myself over in the mirror and at three and a half months, I'd say my body was looking good. Rebel was further along than me and I couldn't wait to get there. My stomach wasn't as big but I sometimes felt like it was.

I got to the church and the parking lot was packed. It never surprised me but this church stayed crowded every Sunday and the amount of cars, appeared to have, doubled. I spoke to a few people on the way in and looked around for a seat. One of the ushers had me follow her and you'll never believe who she had me sit next to. Of course, he was happy and if I didn't know any better, I'd say he set it up. I wasn't gonna complain because it wasn't a tight spot like in some of the other seats.

"You look pretty Ingie." Kiyah was in between us.

"You look better than me. I have to find out who gets you dressed." She started giggling. I reached out to take Miracle but he told me no. She was asleep and he didn't wanna wake her up.

"You look beautiful as always." He leaned in to kiss my cheek and I tried to pull away.

"Ingrid, don't play with me. I'll fuck you right here in this seat." He whispered in my ear. My mouth dropped and I looked around. No one was paying attention but I couldn't believe he said that in church.

"Don't look around. Give me a kiss or I'll hand Miracle to Rebel and make Kiyah go with my mom. I'll sit your pretty ass on my dick and.-"

"Oh my God!" I slammed a kiss on his cheek, just to keep him quiet.

"That was rough. I want a better one." I rolled my eyes. I leaned in and he turned my face as I poked my lips out.

"Tasty lip gloss." He said after placing his lips on mine. At this moment, I was pissed and turned on at the same time.

"Ima handle that wet pussy later." I sucked my teeth and put Kiyah on my lap.

"You need me to say it louder." This time a few people shushed him. I had to laugh because he really didn't care.

****

"How much longer?" Cason stood behind me on the balcony. We were at his moms' house, about to sit for dinner.

"For?"

"For you to be mad? I need some pussy."

108

"You should've gotten it that night."

"Now you tell me." I smacked him on the arm.

"Come here." He grabbed my hand and leaned me against the side of the house.

"I'm so fucking sorry Ingrid. I should've never been there or allowed the temptation, to get as far as she did." I put my head down.

"I went to see her while you were in the hospital to see if her brother was there. She tried to kiss me and I threw her on the ground." I looked up. I never told him about the photo so him mentioning it, made me believe he was telling the truth.

"She was sending me text messages and calling. I was responding to get close. She wouldn't tell me where her brother was and I wanted him. I wanted him so bad, I fucked up. Bae, I swear, I didn't go there to fuck her."

"Cason."

"I promise to never do that shit again. I need you back." He slipped his tongue in my mouth and I happily accepted.

"I need you Ingrid." He kissed my neck and I felt his hand going up my dress.

"Ssss. Shit." His hands were twirling around my pearl.

"Fuck this." He unzipped his pants and let them and his boxers fall to his ankles. He lifted my dress over my ass and thrusted himself inside, making me scratch his back and stifle my scream in his neck.

"Got damn, I missed this. I'm gonna cum." I nodded and shook violently as he forced the orgasm out my body.

"Ahhhhh shit." I felt his seeds shoot inside me.

"I fucking love you Ingrid. I wanna come home." He let me down, made sure my dress was fixed and pulled his clothes up.

"Can I come home?"

"Yea, can he?" I looked up and Rebel was there with Miracle.

"Ummm."

"Ummm what?"

"I'm scared Cason. What if you do it again?" He made me look at him.

"I won't. I'm too scared of losing you forever."

"Awwwww. How cute." I stuck my finger up at Rebel.

"Let me think about it over dinner."

"I'm telling you now if you need more time, I'm cool with that but I'm fucking you tonight." He kissed my lips and walked in the house.

"Bitch, get in the house and wash yo ass."

"How do you know?" I surveyed my clothes.

"The hickey on your neck and your panties are on the ground."

"Oh shit." I snatched and balled them up so no one would see. I went in the house and Cason was walking out the bathroom. He smacked me on the ass and it seemed like everyone stopped and stared. Its no secret, they all wanted us together. I went out to my car and grabbed the bag with me and the girls' clothes in it. I cleaned myself up and changed the girls too.

"You definitely getting thick." Cason came down the steps in some jeans, a t-shirt and Jordan's.

"I meant what I said about digging in that pussy." He pushed me against the wall.

"Lucky for you, she wants you to speak to her." I wrapped my arms around his neck.

"She do huh?" He put my legs on his waist.

"Yea." We started kissing.

"I'm ready to go." He put me down and I stopped him.

"We have to eat."

"Fine." He took my hand and led me up the steps. I heard the door lock in the room and wasted no time getting undressed. We were about to get it in and I gave zero fucks who heard me.

"Eat this pussy Cason and don't stop until I cum three times." I got on all fours and turned around to see him smiling and stroking himself. His face was in my ass and a bitch was in heaven.

"Fuck this." He placed his head under me and had me riding his face. I stopped him, made him scoot up on the bed and turned around so we were in a 69 position. His hands were once again squeezing my ass.

"Mmmmmm, cum for me Cason." I kept jerking and sucking him off.

"Fuck Ingrid. Got damn." His dick was twitching and he was smacking the hell outta my ass.

"Yeaaa. Shit." He came very hard and shook for a second.

"You better had let that go." He said after sticking his finger in my ass and making ne cum on his face.

He lifted me up and had me get back on all fours. He placed both hands on my butt cheeks, separated them and instead of eating, he rammed inside my ass.

"FUCKKKKKKKK!" I screamed out and he arched my back. I gripped the comforter and let the pain subside.

"You better not leave me again. Do I make myself clear?" He pounded faster.

"Yes. YESSSSSSS!" My body became hot and my clit was rock hard.

"I fucking mean it." He grabbed my waist and pumped harder.

"CASONNNNN." I yelled again and came so hard, I fell forward.

"Nah. Get that ass up." He flipped me over and started making love to me.

"I'm so sorry and promise to never mess up again." He hit something and I thought my insides were broken. It hurt and felt good at the same time.

"I love you Cason."

"I love you too." He dug deeper with every stroke.

"Cum with me Ingrid." He stood and put my legs on his shoulder. I felt his hand on my clit and within minutes, both of us were cumming.

Cason

It felt good to not only have sex with my woman but to have her lying in my arms. Once we finished, neither of us moved and wouldn't have if Rebel didn't bang on the door. She was yelling Ingrid was pregnant and needed to eat. I did agree but we both wanted to take a quick nap. However, she wasn't letting us so we got up, showered and joined everyone at the table. Again, they stared and smiled. Well, everyone did except my sister, who hated Ingrid and Rebel for no reason.

Pierce told me about how he got in her ass over the shit at the mall. Selina was and still is dead ass wrong for taking her anger out on Rebel. She didn't even have a reason not to like Ingrid, other than the bullshit stories Rose told her and probably just on the strength Rebel is her best friend. I can say, it didn't bother either of them because once Ingrid made both of us a plate, she sat next to Rebel and conversed like nothing bothered her.

As her man, I knew she was still hurting from the shit I did and sex wasn't gonna make it go away. Time is the only thing and she was going to make me work for her again. I would do anything she wanted to win her back and gave zero fucks on who thought it was crazy. Sometimes men do dumb shit and have to make up in ways he could never imagine.

After everyone was finished eating we all sat around the table and some went into the living room to talk and bullshit. I noticed Selina staring at Rebel, who was paying her no mind. Then she's glance over at Syeed who was deep in a card game with Peirce and a few of my cousins. I stood, walked over to her and snatched her out the chair. Ingrid gave me a weird look and followed me.

"Now what's wrong with you?" Selina was standing there with her arms folded.

"Nothing."

"Man, you not pouting and watching them two for nothing." She sucked her teeth.

"Why the fuck is she out here?" Ingrid stepped out and I pulled her in front of me.

"Because she's my woman and this is a free country."

"Selina, keep the fucking attitude."

"This is the shit I'm talking about Cason. You never let Desi speak to me that way." I felt Ingrid tense up and she had every right to. Selina was being malicious for no reason.

"Desi is my past and you mentioning her, was strictly to hurt Ingrid. So tell me right fucking now what the problem is and don't bring up no stupid shit about Syeed."

"Why does he still love her?" She plopped down on one of the chairs.

"Did he tell you that?"

"No but I can see it in his eyes, every time he looks at her."

"Are you serious?" Ingrid butted in.

"Look at him." She pointed to Syeed. He was no longer in his seat and looking around the house.

"Rebel, is sitting on Pierce's lap so its clear he's not looking for her." Ingrid stood in front of her.

"I won't ever fuck with you in a friend level Selina but I can tell you, that man loves you. The way he had his arm around you at the table and how he caters to you."

"Its because I'm pregnant."

"No. Its because regardless of how the two of you met, he's in love with you." Ingrid sat next to her.

"Rebel was his first love and vice versa so its natural for him to still love her. In fact, he always will, just like you'll always have a place in your heart for your first love." Selina sat there listening to her.

"Syeed messed up and you know they say everything happens for a reason. God pushed Rebel outta his life so he could find his true love."

"I don't know."

"Its not for you to know but if you keep treating him like the enemy, he will leave."

"Don't tell her shit. Let his ass leave her miserable ass."

"CASON!"

"Fuck that." She told me to be quiet. Ingrid was better than me because I wouldn't be saying two words to her.

"Selina, I can tell you Rebel is no threat to your relationship. She is crazy in love with Pierce. Shit, sometimes it scares me how much they're so much alike. I think, they'll end up killing each other for something stupid at times." I had to agree. Those two were rough, yet loved the hell outta each other.

"Selina, you ok?" Syeed walked over and checked her.

"Yea. I was just having a moment." Ingrid stood up.

"I hope you weren't out here talking about old shit again. I told you, I'm out if you can't' move past it." She looked at Ingrid, who looked at me. I was about to tell him.

"Let's go Cason."

"Hell no. She.-" I watched Ingrid lick her lips and then put her index finger in her mouth.

"You play too much. Bring your ass in the house before we go back upstairs."

"Who says I don't want to?" She took my hand and made me go in with her. I wanted to see Syeed get in Selina's ass.

"Cason, someone is outside looking for you." One of my cousins said.

"I'm going to the bathroom." She kissed my lips and I went to see who it was.

****

"Ima ask you one time and if you don't give me a good answer, I promise to lay you the fuck out." I told Marsha who popped up at my mom's.

"I wanna see Kiyah." I busted out laughing.

"I'm serious Cason. I haven't seen her in months."

"Not my problem."

"Desi, would not appreciate how you're behaving." Is today bring up Desi day or something? Why the hell does everyone keep mentioning her?

"Nah, what she wouldn't appreciate is all the bullshit you've done since she passed."

"I didn't wanna have to do this but you leave me no choice." She handed me a piece of paper and it appeared to be Desi's handwriting. It was dated to four years ago.

Dear Cason,

I don't know how to tell you this and I hope you never get this letter. I'm only writing it to clear my conscience. A few years back, when you cheated on me, I slept with someone else. He and I, shared many nights together and unfortunately; we didn't use protection. When you promised never to cheat on me again and I took you back, we made love and conceived Kiyah. Well, I think we did, which is why I'm writing this letter. In my heart, Kiyah is a hundred percent yours but there's still doubt that she may not be. I'm sorry, I couldn't tell you. Wow! Writing this really lifted a weight off my chest. Again, I hope this letter never finds you. Desi

"What type of shit is this?"

"I told you, she may not be yours in the courtroom but you never believed me. I filed a motion to have a DNA test conducted on Kiyah. You will get the paperwork in the mail. If by some miracle she isn't yours, I promise to keep her away

121

from you forever." She ran to her car and left me standing there confused and angry.

"Cason, what's wrong?" I heard Ingrid ask.

"Nothing."

"Baby, you have a few tears falling down your face." I wiped them quickly.

"I said, I'm fine."

"Are you sure? I've never seen you this upset."

"I FUCKING SAID I WAS FINE. GET THE FUCK OUT MY FACE." I shouted. She jumped and backed up. The fear on Ingrid's face would be etched in my brain forever.

"What the hell is going on out here?" My mom came out.

"I'm leaving." She stormed off in the house.

"GO!"

"Cason Hill, why are you speaking to her that way?"

"Man, I'm out." I went inside, snatched my keys and peeled out the driveway. I needed some time to myself. I drove to the cemetery and walked to Desi's grave. Some dude was standing there and tried to run, when he noticed me. I tackled his ass to the ground and pulled my gun out.

"Who the fuck are you?"

"Please don't kill me." He was shook.

"Who the fuck are you?"

"I knew Desi and.-" I pulled him up.

"Did you fuck her?" I had to know if this cornball, is the one she slept with.

"She said, she didn't have a boyfriend. I'm sorry."

"Did...you...fuck...her?" I said it slowly in case he couldn't understand fucking English. Its clear he could because he's black but he didn't answer my question.

"Only a few times."

"Did you use condoms?" He put his head down and that confirmed my suspicion.

"SHIT!" I put my hands on top of my head.

"I didn't know she had anyone. Do you know where her daughter is?" I put the gun to his forehead.

"That's my fucking daughter."

"Are you sure?"

123

"Nigga, you want me to kill you?"

"I'm sorry. This lady who claimed to be Desi's mom, tracked me down and said it's a possibility she's mine. I never wanted kids and still don't."

"So why you wanna know?"

"This woman said she'd pay me fifty thousand dollars to take a DNA test and if the baby is mine, she'll pay me to keep her."

"WHAT?"

"Look man. I don't want any problems and I damn sure wouldn't give my daughter, if that's her, to a woman who is willing to pay. Something is shady about her and I'll be damned if she gets anywhere near her."

"When did you speak to her?"

"About a month ago. She had the courthouse send me a subpoena to take the test."

"What do you want?"

"I don't want anything. Desi and I, were careless and she knew I didn't want any kids. Hell, its why she went back to you after all the cheating."

124

"Hold up. Desi, told you about us?"

"She said her man cheated too many times and she was fed up. We spoke a lot and the few times we did hook up, I made sure to tell her, we couldn't be together because I didn't want kids. She understood and even though I pulled out each time, its still a chance the little girl could be mine from what the lady said." I blew my breath out.

"Look my daughter is three and Desi's mother has been causing major problems. I don't wanna get a test but if we're both ordered by the court to get one, it is, what it is. I'm telling you now, I'm not giving her up. She has a stepmother who won't allow it either."

"Here. Take my card." I looked down and this nigga is a fucking lawyer. *Just my luck.*

"I'll have some papers drawn up to state, if the little girl is mine, you can remain on the birth certificate and acknowledged as her father. I will relinquish any rights to her and if possible, keep the information hidden. All I ask is you keep that woman away from her."

"I'll have my lawyer call you tomorrow." He ran to his car and left me standing there staring at Desi's tombstone. I wanted to destroy it and erase her from being Kiyah's mother.

I understand the cheating but to let a nigga fuck you raw is unacceptable. Yea, he pulled out but it doesn't change the possibility. I got in my car and left with plans to never return. I can forgive a lot of things but to have another nigga be my daughters father, I can't. I'm gonna get Marsha too. This bitch has gone too far and its time to reap, what she sow.

Rebel

"What happened?" Cason's mom was asking Ingrid as she packed the girls up to leave.

"To be honest, I don't know. We made up, as I'm sure you all know. He went to talk to Selina, we came in and one of his cousins said there was someone looking for him. I went to the bathroom and when I opened the front door, no one was out there with him. He was leaning on the side with a few tears coming down his face. I asked was he ok and he snapped. I love Cason but there's absolutely no way, I can be around him like that. I swear, Roger is all I saw when he shouted in my face." She sat on the bed and broke down crying.

"I wonder who was outside."

"So do I. I'll be back." His mom closed the door and Ingrid rested her head on my shoulder.

"Am I stupid for making up with him?"

"Ingrid, no man is perfect and what you do is your business."

"I know but what if it happens again?"

"Again, your business is yours. My mom always says, only you will know when you had enough. Don't let outsiders dictate what you should accept because most of them accepted a lot more. Listen." She looked at me.

"I'm not excusing him snapping on you but whoever came to that door pissed him off bad. Unfortunately, you felt the wrath of it because you found him. I doubt he meant to take it out on you especially; knowing what you've been through. When he calms down, I bet he begs for your forgiveness. I'm not saying to give it to him but I will say listen to whatever it is and base your choice off that. Shit, for all we know Odessa could've been out there and told him she had AIDS."

"REBEL!"

"What? You never know with these broke bitches. Look at Selina. She swears somebody wants Syeed."

"Do you?"

"HELL NO! And even if I did, it would only be to get back at her."

"You never told me why you wouldn't take him back. You said people accept what they want."

"Ingrid, I could get past the cheating if it were one time. This nigga fucked her more than once and then got her pregnant. I can tolerate a lot but a baby? I'm good."

"Yea if Cason had a baby on me I'd definitely leave."

"That nigga ain't having no kids by anyone else. The way you two were moaning all loud and shit, I'd say y'all strung out."

"You heard us?" She covered her mouth.

"Mostly you but I heard him right before I knocked."

"We definitely have great sex." She picked Miracle up and opened the door. Kiyah and Tiffany were running down the hallway.

"Kiyah are you staying with your grandmother?"

"Yes." She hugged Ingrid. I went down the steps and walked her outside.

"You ready?" He put his arms on my belly.

"Ready for some dick."

"And trust, it's ready for you."

****

"What up Rebel?" I turned around and Syeed was coming outta the jewelry store. I only came here to grab a pair of baby Jordan's I wanted. We still didn't know what we were having but I had to get them.

"Goodbye."

"Wait!" He touched my arm.

"I just wanna say I'm sorry from the bottom of my heart. I never meant to hurt you." He ran his hand down my face.

"It's fine and you already said it."

"You're still beautiful and I'm glad to see you're happy."

"Thanks and I really am. He's a little rough around the edges but I love him."

"Rough ain't the word."

"Don't talk about my man." We both started laughing.

"That nigga crazy but I can tell he loves you."

"Shit, he better after knocking me up."

"Can you believe our kids will be related?"

"I know right. Who knew?"

"Rebel, don't let Selina get to you."

"I'm not but I am gonna whoop her ass for the stunt she pulled at the movies." He shook his head laughing.

"She knows I will always love you and feels threatened."

"Did you ever cheat on her?"

"Surprisingly no. I didn't even plan on doing it to you. I think it was hard for me to move past what we had because of the hurt and pain I caused. Then, I never got to apologize. She thinks it's because I still want you."

"Do you?"

"Not at all. Believe it or not, I believe she and I were supposed to meet. She is the only woman I want and that's some real shit."

I was pissed. Not because they were together but because he never cheated and loved her more than me. It makes me think he never really loved me. How could he, if he cheating while he was with me, came easy but he can't fathom doing the same to her.

"I'm happy for you Syeed. It took me a long time to forgive you but I think you apologizing helped. Thank you." He reached out and gave me a hug. However, this bitch was in her feelings.

"I fucking knew it." She stormed over and smacked him across the face.

"Yo, What the fuck?" He grabbed her hand.

"Why the hell were you hugging her? Did y'all hook up? I'm sick of you two."

"And I told you if you didn't stop with the jealousy shit, I'm out."

"Every time I turn around you're with her."

"Save those bullshit ass lies. Besides today we've only spoken at the movies."

"So why were you just hugging her?"

"It doesn't matter because I'm done. I'll be at the house to get my shit." He walked off mad as hell. She had the dumbest look on her face.

"Just so you know Selina." I moved closer.

132

"He apologized for the past and guess what?" She sucked her teeth.

"All he talked about was being happy with you. He felt like fate put you together and he couldn't fathom cheating on you. But you're so dam insecure you just lost a good man for nothing. I have my man and rude or not, he makes me very happy." Now it was my turn to leave her standing there looking stupid.

I finished doing more shopping and drove home. My feet were hurting and so was my back. I was already six and a half months and the time was flying by. Pierce kept saying I could pop any day and I agreed. However, the doctor said even though the baby could survive at this point, it's always better to keep it in my stomach for as long as possible.

"Hey baby." I kissed Pierce when he opened the door.

"Hey."

"How much shit you buy?"

"Not too much."

"Whatever." He went to take the things out and I took off upstairs to start a bath. I removed all my clothes and got right in.

"I'm hungry."

"Aren't you always? What you want?" He pulled his phone out to order. After he finished I grabbed his arm so he wouldn't leave.

"Babe, let me tell you what happened at the mall." I filled him in on everything and he just shook his head.

"At least, he apologized."

"Yea, I guess."

"You're not mad about us hugging, are you?"

"I trust you Rebel. And you know I won't have a problem killing you if I thought something else was going on. Like I said before; that's her insecurities and it's her fault, he left her." He leaned over and kissed me.

"Now hurry up out this tub. You use way too much water in here." I grabbed his shirt and pulled him in with me.

"Dammit Reb."

"Gimme a kiss." All I'm gonna say is, he stripped and gave me exactly what I wanted.

Shayla

"He hasn't been to this strip club since we got in town." Melanie whined. She's one of the chicks, Sway sent up here to get Pierce. I wish, I knew where him and that bitch lived because I'd take both of them out.

"He'll come out eventually." I picked my drink up and glanced around the club. There were some fine men in here but none I was interested in.

"Fuck it. I'm gonna dance." She went on the dance floor and she may as well, danced naked. Her dress was now over her ass and you could see her pussy, clear as day and her chest was falling out the top of it.

"Sway, would kill her if saw this shit." Essence said and sat back down shaking her head.

"Look over there." I pointed to Cason and Pierce, coming through the door.

"DAMN!! Both of them are sexy." She was drooling.

"Which one is who?" I hated to point Pierce out because he damn sure looked sexy as hell. Both of them were dressed in black with diamonds dripping. They usually don't show off too much so I'm shocked to see them with that much jewelry on. I noticed Cason looking around and then shake hands with a few guys. They must be here on business.

"Pierce is the one without dreads." This bitch licked her lips. I wanted to smack her but this is a job we had to do. I made her get Melanie because if either of them saw me, I'd be dead on sight.

"What's up?" This bitch pulled her dress down and had to catch her breath. What the hell was she doing?

"Look. Pierce and Cason are here. Both of you know what to do." They fixed themselves up and casually strolled to where they were.

There were rules to how Sway wanted a job done. For example, they are to make themselves known but not in a loud, ghetto or ratchet way. We weren't allowed to dress like a ho. Even though Essence made sure to wear her clothes tight, they would still be decent. You can never get too drunk because

Sway didn't want you to get caught slipping or mentioning what you were really doing. At last but not least; never, ever, let these guys fuck you raw. If anyone popped up pregnant or even caught a disease, that's your ass. I guess when the boss fucks you without a condom, he expects a clean pussy.

I know it sounds crazy but all of us were on a form of birth control because of it. Yea, Sway had a girl or should I say wife and didn't want her to find out, he's fucking around. He claims she makes a ton of accusations but since none of us pop up pregnant or he doesn't give her a disease she can't prove it. Mind you, he has six kids and only two are by her.

Anyway, I watched the two of them hit the bar and every one of the dudes had their eye on them; except Pierce and Cason. It was crazy because both women were gorgeous. I'm not about to describe them but just know, Sway don't fuck with ugly women. I sent a text and told them to figure out a way to be noticed. Sure enough, Melanie whispered in the bartenders' ear and a few minutes later. I saw the woman place an Ace of Spades bottle in front of them. They looked and it was all it took.

Pierce let his eyes roam up and down Melanie, and Essence stepped in front of Cason. Of course, I couldn't hear a damn thing but from the way the girls were laughing and making sexual faces, it's safe to assume everything's good. I finished my drink and disappeared in the crowd to leave. I'll meet them at the hotel and we'll go from there.

****

"Hey ma." I walked in my mothers' house and found her in the kitchen.

"Where the fuck you been?" She turned around with an evil glare on her face.

"I've only been gone a few weeks." Actually, I wasn't sure how long its been. Between working and trying to figure out ways to get my baby daddy, I didn't pay it any mind.

"A few weeks huh? What about your fucking daughter?"

"Ma, I knew she was ok with Pierce." The last day I saw her was at the hospital. Pierce wouldn't let me take her after that day.

"Tiffany has been asking for you every time I see her and you walk in here, without a care in the world."

"Ma, I had to get away."

"Why?"

"I tried to kill Pierce's girlfriend." She had a shocked look on her face.

"WHAT?"

"I couldn't let her live after the fight and.-"

"You couldn't let her live? When did you become a killer? Or even some ratchet girl?" She wiped her hands on the apron.

"What happened to you?"

"Nothing. I'm just trying to make a better life for me and my daughter."

"By attempting to murder someone? I don't know what's gotten into you but your gonna end up like that Rose woman. I heard what Cason did to her." I wonder what he did. She walked over to me.

"Honey." Her hands were on both sides of my face.

"If you don't stop this reckless behavior, he's going to kill you and where would that leave Tiffany." Just as I was about to respond my daughter came in the kitchen. Once she saw me, she jumped in my arms and all she talked about was some damn Rebby and her daddy. How the hell is she missing me, when they're pretending to be the perfect family over there?

"You should be ashamed of yourself." My mom was talking shit and I was letting it go in one ear and out the other. I stood and lifted Tiffany with me.

"Where are you going?" I grabbed my things and Tiffany's hand.

"I'm taking her out."

"Shayla, let her father know."

"For what? She's my daughter."

"Ok but he specifically told me not to let her go with you unless he knew. Look, I don't want to get in the middle of y'all shit so don't put me in it. If you want to take her, just call him."

"Fine!" I picked my phone up and dialed his number.

141

"I'll be right there." He answered without me speaking. My mom looked at me.

"DADDY!" Tiffany shouted.

"I'm taking her out Pierce. You can pick her up later." I headed towards the door.

"If you step outside that house, I promise you'll get hit." I looked around and no one was out there but it didn't mean, no one was watching.

"Yea, right. If you had people watching my mom's, they would've took a shot when I got here."

"You have to be the dumbest bitch I know."

"What?" I lifted my daughter up and walked to my car. He won't allow anyone to shoot while I'm holding her.

"I knew you were there. I was outta town and no one has come in because I told them not to. I'll be there soon." He hung up.

I sat Tiffany on my lap and told her to pretend she's driving. Again, he won't allow anyone to bother me. The only thing is, he'll know where I'm at. I didn't see any vehicles following me until I put her on the passenger side at the light. I put her seatbelt on and weaved in and outta traffic. The car was keeping up with me but at a slow speed. I guess they didn't want to cause an accident. In my eyes, it worked out because not too long after, no one was behind me.

It took me a long time to get where I needed and the person wasn't too happy to see me. This was one of his vacation houses and where he fucked us, on occasions. He opened the door and allowed me to lay Tiffany in the bedroom. After taking her shoes off and placing her under the covers, I stepped out the room, only to be met with a closed fist to the face. The shit knocked me against the wall.

"Why the fuck are you here and with this kid?" After I regained the strength to stand, I walked in the kitchen to grab some ice.

"I wanted to see my daughter and he planned on keeping her away. Sway, I know we're supposed to be working but I miss her."

"And that's my problem how?" He gave me the evilest look ever.

"Its not." I put my head down after applying the ice.

"When she wakes up, you need to go." He had his hand under my shirt and was about to put the other one in my jeans.

"What is going on out here?" Some woman said and out walked his wife.

"Shayla was having man problems and brought her daughter here."

"I don't give a fuck. She has to go." The woman stood there with her arms folded. We've never met the wife and now that I have, I can already tell she's a bitch. I looked at Sway and he didn't say a word.

"Really, Sway?" He shrugged his shoulders.

"Really, what? Bitch, I said you have to go, so bounce."

"Bitch."

"You heard me."

"Am I bitch, when I fuck your nigga?" Her mouth dropped and she stared at him.

"GET THE FUCK OUT!" I walked past them and went in the room to grab Tiffany. I heard mad shit breaking in the other room.

144

"Goodbye." I tried to walk past and felt my hair being pulled and fell. My daughter woke up screaming because her head bounced off the floor.

"You fucking bitch." I hopped up and swung, hitting her in the face. My daughter was screaming and his wife was cursing at the same time she was hitting me. I'm no fighter but I'm not gonna allow no bitch to hit me either. His wife had the nerve to be swinging her arms like a windmill. The least he could've done was get her boxing lessons. I heard a gunshot go off and froze.

"Get the fuck out before I shoot this kid in the head."

"OH MY GOD!" There was a hole in the floor, next to my daughter. Her eyes were rolling and her body was shaking. I snatched her up and ran to my car. I put her in the backseat and turned my GPS on to find the closest hospital. Unfortunately, it was twenty minutes away.

By the time I got there, Tiffany wasn't breathing and her face was blue. I ran in screaming with her in my arms. The doctors and nurses came rushing out and took her away. I could see blood dripping from the back of her skull. Did she hit the floor that hard? Pierce, is going to fucking kill me. I sat there in a zone waiting for the doctors to return and when he did, I almost passed out from what he told me. When I got it together, I made the dreadful phone call to her father.

Pierce

"What the fuck you mean, you lost her?" I asked the dude who was watching Shayla's mom house. I knew she'd be back eventually to see Tiffany but I had no idea she'd take my daughter.

"She was weaving in an outta traffic. Pierce, your daughter was sitting in the front seat. If I kept going, she would've sped up more and lost control of the car. I didn't wanna risk it. I'm sorry."

"Nah man. My bad. Fuck!" I picked my phone up and dialed Reb. She's the only one at this moment who could calm me down.

"Hey baby." She sounded tired as hell.

"I need you to meet me at Shayla's mom house."

"What's wrong? Is it Tiffany? Is she ok?" I could hear the concern in her voice. Her and Tiffany were like two peas in a pod.

"I'll tell you when you get here. And Reb."

"Yea. I'm coming."

"Take your time."

"Pierce you're making me nervous. Where is she?"

"Ma. Take your time getting here. I don't want you getting into an accident." She never responded. I stood out there talking to the guys, hoping Shayla would bring Tiffany home.

"Pierce I'm sorry. I told her to call you." Her mom was crying.

"It's ok." She gave me a hug.

"I hope nothing happened to her." I snapped my neck to look at her.

"Why would you say that?"

"I don't know. Shayla told me, she tried to kill your girlfriend and how you may want to kill her. And she mentioned trying to make a better life for Tiffany. What could she possibly be doing out there?" I didn't even respond because my phone rang from Shayla.

"What up?" I had to remain calm if I planned on finding her. I'ma ring her neck, once I see her.

148

"Pierce, ummm." I heard nervousness in her voice, which made my instincts kick right in.

"Where's Tiffany?"

"Pierce, I didn't do it."

"Do what?" Now she was aggravating me.

"You need to come out to The University Hospital in Maryland."

"WHAT! Why the fuck are you in Maryland?"

"Pierce, hurry up." She hung the phone up and I ran to my car with everyone else behind me. Rebel pulled up, just as I was getting in.

"Hey Baby. Where's Tiffany?" She waddled over to me.

"Do you need the bathroom?"

"No, I'm ok." She looked around me and waved to Shayla's mom. The two of them spoke a lot, since she's the one who dropped Tiffany off.

Shit, if it weren't for Rebel, my daughter would never see her. She had to remind me that what Shayla is doing or has done, doesn't have anything to do with her mom. It's the truth but I still wasn't tryna hear it. Her mom appreciated it for sure

149

and always made sure to let us know, if she left the house with her and where they were at all times. She always said, she wants to stay in her granddaughters' life, even if Shayla won't.

"Pierce?"

"I'll tell you on the way." I helped her in the car, tossed her keys to Jeff and asked him to drive her car home. Of course, he was happy because she drove the Maserati.

"You better not crash it Jeff." She told him.

"Man, go head."

"Jeff."

"I got it Rebel. But I am going to drive the shit outta it." She turned to look at me and I shrugged my shoulders. Jeff has been asking to drive her car for the longest. She rolled her eyes and sat back in the car.

"You're buying me a new one if he crashes it."

"Hell, if I am."

"PIERCE!"

"Alright damn. Such a damn baby." She smirked and asked me to tell her what was going on.

By the time I finished, she had tears running down her face. We didn't even know the extent of what happened but to know she's hurt, is enough. The remainder of the ride was quiet and once we got there, both of us couldn't get in the door fast enough. I spotted that dumb bitch on the phone. Rebel, took my hand in hers and squeezed it tight.

"Why is she here?" Now it was my turn to squeeze Rebel's hand.

"Where's Tiffany?" I bypassed her attitude and question.

"I'm not telling you shit with this bitch standing here." Rebel took her hand and karate chopped Shayla in the throat. I busted out laughing and walked to the nurses' station. Shayla was trying her hardest to catch her breath. She better be happy that's all Rebel did; for now.

"Hi. My name is Pierce Hill and my daughter Tiffany.-"

"Oh, you're her father." The woman cut me off.

"Duh! Isn't that what I said?" Reb, pinched my arm.

"What? Shit, I started off with my daughter is here. She should.-"

"Ok, Pierce. I'm sorry about him. He's just nervous because we received a call about her being here but nothing else."

"Its ok, I understand. The reason I asked is because another guy was here and asked about her too." She pointed to Sway. I took my piece out my back pocket and Rebel stood in front of me.

"Pierce, not here."

"Reb, I'm sure he's the one who sent her to kill you and.-"

"Pierce, look at me." She made me look at her. Sway was standing there on the phone grinning.

"I know its hard baby but we still don't know what's going on with Tiffany. If you act up, you'll get thrown out or arrested. Come on. We'll deal with him later." She pushed me back. The nurse walked us in another room.

"Listen." She closed the door.

"I don't know what's going on with that woman but whoever the man is, apologized for what happened and told her she better not tell the child's father." My blood was boiling as she told me the two of them were arguing so loud they had to get security. What the hell is she doing arguing with him and my daughter is here, hurt?

"What happened to my daughter?"

"Hold on."

"Rebel, she better be ok." I sat down and felt her hands massaging my shoulders.

"She's gonna be fine." I pulled her on my lap and moved the hair out her face.

"I love you Reb and from here on out, you'll be Tiffany's mom."

"Pierce." She tried to respond but the doctor walked in.

"Hi. I'm Doctor Moore and I'm the pediatrician on duty." He took a seat and Rebel sat on the couch.

"Is she ok?" The door opened and Shayla walked in.

"Baby, relax." I swear if Rebel wasn't here. I'd shoot this bitch on sight.

"Unfortunately, Tiffany is in a medically induced coma."

"WHAT?" I couldn't hold out any longer. My hands were wrapped around Shayla's throat.

"PIERCE PLEASE STOP! YOU'RE GONNA MAKE ME GO IN LABOR AND ITS TOO EARLY!" I heard Rebel screaming in my ear and after seeing Shayla turn blue, I dropped her. The doctor was petrified and my girl had tears running down my face.

"FUCK!" I started pacing the floor.

"Is everything ok in here?" The same nurse had come in.

"Nah, its not." I grabbed Shayla's hair and literally drug her out the hospital door, kicking and screaming. People were staring at me and I didn't give a fuck.

"Pierce, what's going on?" I saw my mom and her boyfriend Charles, my aunt, uncle and Cason coming in the door. I forgot my girl called them on the way.

"I'm going to kill this bitch."

"Aight Pierce. Let her go." My uncle took my hands off her and pushed me in the hospital. Security was coming in our direction.

"Yo, that woman almost killed his daughter. She's not allowed back in here. Do I make myself clear?" Cason barked out and the dude was nervous as hell. You could hear him on the radio telling someone to make sure the exits are secure, described what Shayla had on and not to let her reenter. Everyone followed behind me in the room.

"What's wrong with her?" I ran to Rebel's side. The doctor was checking her vitals and he had a wet paper towel on her forehead.

"She had a panic attack and started to hyperventilate."

"What the fuck you panicking for?" My mother smacked me on the back of the head and my aunt let me have it.

"She's gonna need to rest."

"She will. I grabbed her hand and sat down.

"As I was saying about your daughter." Cason closed the door.

"Her mother claimed she fell and hit her head, which is why there's a huge knot on the back. There was a gash in it and we had to give her five stiches. The reason she's in a coma is.-"

"COMA!" My mom and aunt shouted at the same time.

"She's in a medically induced coma because a child at her age, suffering that amount of head trauma is harmful."

"What do you mean?"

"She had a lot of swelling on her brain and being she's still growing, it can affect her motor skills."

"Are you saying she's going to be special needs?" My mom asked and all I could do was wish, I killed Shayla sooner.

"I'm not saying that at all. However; I have to tell you the possibilities. She may or may not have amnesia and once she wakes up, we'll do a test to make sure she's not paralyzed."

"Come again."

"I'm sorry sir but when your daughter fell on the floor; besides hitting her head she fell on something that pinched a nerve in her back." I could feel the tears falling down my face.

"Listen. I know this is a lot to take in and I can't imagine what you're going through. And these things may not happen but like I said before; as a doctor, I have to inform you." He stood up.

"Would you like to see her?"

"Yes."

The walk to the pediatric ICU floor was dreadful and quiet. None of us spoke a word and once we walked in, you could see the somber look on the nurses' face. Evidently, Tiffany was the only one in there and they felt sorry for her. I mean, it's the way I took it. He led us in the room and I almost broke down seeing her like that. Tubes were everywhere and the bandage around her head, only made me angrier. He told us what every tube was for, the tests they were going to run and that, he'll give her medicine to take her out the coma when they run another MRI to make sure the swelling went down. Talk about a nigga devastated, you can't even imagine.

Everyone found a seat and I had Rebel sit in the so-called mommy's chair. I wasn't being smart but she's pregnant and it's the most comfortable one there. It pulled out and the nurse brought her a blanket. I knew she wasn't going anywhere and knowing her, she'd be asleep shortly. The nurse asked if anyone needed anything and after bringing my mom and aunt a blanket, with some coffee, she left.

"What happened?" Charles asked.

He was cool as hell and my uncle's best friend. They've been together for about ten years but were never married. My mom said as long as he didn't cheat on her, she wouldn't leave him. But she was never getting married. My pops did her dirty and she refused to be stuck. Charles said he didn't care and made her wear a ring. If you ask me, I think they went to the justice of peace to get it done. Ain't nobody wearing pretend rings. I don't care what they say.

"Shayla did this." I started telling them everything when a woman dressed in a suit came in. All of us knew exactly who she was. The doctor told us child services had to come.

"Hello everyone. I'm Mrs. Houston and I'm sorry we had to meet under these circumstances."

"You're not taking my daughter." Rebel said and no one corrected her.

"Are you her mom?"

"From this day forward, I am." I smiled and so did everyone else.

"Ok, well, let me be clear on what's going to happen." You could tell she was a no nonsense woman.

"The birth mother will no longer be allowed around her, until we do a thorough investigation. She will be placed under the dad's custody and if you would like your name on any paperwork, go down to the courthouse and start the process."

"What process?"

"The child's birth mother is downstairs right now, speaking to police and trying to get you arrested for assault." I looked at her.

"I don't really care what happened and if you did it for your daughter, then I don't blame you. This little girl suffered a lot and there's no way in hell, I'd allow her to take Tiffany out of this hospital. Now, if you're claiming to be her mom from this day forward, he will need to put you down as either the wife, next of kin or something. Otherwise; she'll be awarded to the state if no one in the family takes her."

"Her being my fiancé, isn't enough?"

"I'm afraid its not. People get engaged all the time and who's to say, they'll stick around." We all looked at her.

"I know all relationships don't work but a marriage is easier to deal with, in the eyes of the law."

"Ok. What do we need to do?" She stayed in the room for over two hours, interviewing all of us and giving us the steps to go through to make sure Shayla never gets Tiffany again. She won't have to worry about that because I damn sure will get rid of her, soon as my daughter wakes up.

Rebel

I was heartbroken when Pierce told me Tiffany was hurt. It didn't help to see her lying in the bed with all those tubes going in her. I couldn't help but blame myself. He didn't want Shayla's mom to have her alone and I told him, it ain't her fault Shayla's crazy. It took a lot of persuading to make him agree. The first day he dropped her off, he stayed outside the house until it was time to go to bed. Eventually, he got used to it and called every few hours to check on her. If he went outta town, he'd make sure someone was available at all times to keep an eye on her.

After about a month of the bitch not returning, he started easing up and felt more comfortable. However, over the last week he knew something was up. He wouldn't tell me what because he said I couldn't be stressing his kid out. I wanted to know anyway and went through his phone. There wasn't much going on but a phone number was on there a lot and no name was attached. We all know it was a bitch and I called it a few times and no one ever answered. I found it to be weird, especially; when the call log said they'd speak for five or ten minutes at a time.

I was going to address it but him and Cason went outta town on some business shit. I could accuse him of cheating but he never let my call got to voicemail and if I called in the middle of the night, he'd answer and twice, we face timed and had phone sex. If there was another woman, she was stupid as hell. I'll be damned if I'm with a dude and he answered while we were together.

"What you doing?" He was texting away on his cell.

"Work shit."

"Work shit, huh?" He looked up. I've never questioned him about his job.

"Say what's on your mind." I stood up and walked over to him. We were at the hospital now for a week and Tiffany was still in the coma. The swelling had gone down and tomorrow the doctor was giving her medication to come out.

"This is on my mind." I snatched the phone out his hand.

"Yo! What the fuck?" He tried to take it back. I didn't get to read a lot but the few messages I did see, were enough. Whoever the chick was mentioned them meeting up right before Tiffany got hurt and she missed speaking to him.

"Its not what you think Reb." I threw the phone at him.

"You meeting up with her, is not what I think? She's missing you nigga so that means something's going on." I walked over to pick my things up.

"Reb, I swear its not.-"

"Are you trying to pay me back for not telling you what I did?"

"What? Hell no. I don't do no revenge shit."

"Then why are you texting and seeing another woman? I'm supposed to be your fiancé and if its not what I think, then I should've known."

"I was gonna tell you."

"Did you fuck her?"

"Fuck no."

"Did she suck your dick?"

"You bugging." At least, no sex happened.

163

"Did you kiss her?" He let his hand roam over his head.

"Let me get this right." I took my phone out and sent for an Uber. I was going to stay in a hotel because I didn't have a car to go home and I wasn't leaving Tiffany.

"You kissed a woman, knowing you have a pregnant fiancé. You're meeting up with her, sending messages and most likely going to see her again. Is that about right?" He stood there with a dumb look on his face.

"Then you sit here in my face responding to her, like that ain't disrespectful. Have you been talking to her on the phone while we been here?"

"Where you going?" Him ignoring my question, only confirmed what I knew.

"I don't care what you're doing when it comes to your job but when you involve other women and disrespecting me, I'm tapping out."

"So its ok for you to do the job you had but not me?" I walked over to him. The door was open and we were already getting loud. These people didn't need to know our business. I was embarrassed enough that whoever this woman was could get a laugh, even though she wasn't here.

"I admitted to being wrong for not telling you, I did. But I never slept with anyone, nor did I kiss them when we were together. Regardless; it was wrong and I should've told you. I never thought you'd try and get me back." I shook my head in disbelief.

"Why did you propose?" I folded my arms.

"What you mean?" His phone started to ring.

"Why did you ask me to marry you?"

"I love you Rebel and you're the only woman I wanna spend the rest of my life with." He tried to hug me and I smacked his arms away.

"You contradicted every word out your mouth because if you felt that way, no job would make you cheat." He stared at me.

"Texting, calling and spending time with another woman is cheating. And you know damn well, kissing is. The only thing left to do is fuck." I wiped the tears falling down my face. The thought of allowing a woman to be as close as she is, hurts me bad. All I wanted to do is kill him.

"I believed ever word you told me about your feelings. Now, in my eyes, you're a fucking liar and I hope she's worth you losing me over." I walked over to Tiffany and kissed her forehead. I took the ring off and placed it on the chair. The nigga fucking lost it and tossed me against the wall.

"Put…it…back…on." He had my shirt balled up in his hands.

"Sir." One of the nurses called out.

"GET THE FUCK OUT!" I nodded to her and she backed up. He wouldn't hurt me but I knew he couldn't take me leaving.

"You did this Pierce. Now let me go."

"Rebel, I swear you better put the fucking ring back on."

"For what? Huh? You to continue doing shit with another woman. You lost your damn mind. Get off me." I pushed him and he gripped my shirt tighter.

166

"You think, I'm playing." He took his gun out and placed it on the side of my head.

"We're in this for life. Now put the fucking ring on."

"PIERCE! WHAT THE FUCK YOU DOING?" Cason snatched him away and all I could do is shake my head. I fixed my clothes, walked up and smacked the fuck outta him.

"How fucking dare you cheat on me and try to make me stay with you? You did this Pierce? You fucked us up. Deal with it."

"When did you cheat?" Cason still had him backed in a corner.

"Rebel, you better not walk out."

"Go find the bitch who has your time." Cason still looked confused.

"Oh and if she pops up pregnant, you can forget about my child. The only sibling my kid has, is Tiffany. Stupid ass nigga." I walked out and could hear him yelling. He got me fucked up.

****

"Hey boo! You good?" Ingrid asked. She came out here to pick me up. Its been two weeks, since the blow up with Pierce. Tiffany woke up three days ago and I refused to go up there, until he left. His mom called and told me she made Cason take him out, so I could see her. Tiffany kept asking where I was.

When I saw her, she reached out and I started crying. Not only was she out the coma but the doctor said she had no paralysis and as of right now, her motor skills and everything was fine. He told us she could go home in a few days, which is today. The reason Ingrid came is because I had no way home and I wasn't riding with him. Plus, she just came from the hospital from seeing Tiffany. Kiyah and her were ecstatic to see each other.

"I'm ok. You ready?" I picked Miracle up and she took Kiyah by the hand and my small luggage I purchased. The day I left the hospital, I went to Walmart to buy clothes and any other things I needed. It was only stretch pants and t-shirts for me at this point anyway. The ride was long but the kids fell asleep, which is a good thing.

"You wanna get something to eat?" She asked when we pulled into Chili's.

"How you asking and already here?"

"Shit, I would've gotten my food to go." She laughed and we both got out to get the kids. We walked in and it was a little crowded. The hostess sat us in a booth and said the waiter would be over.

"Hi. Are you Rebel?" Some chick asked. She was very pretty and her body is how mine was before getting pregnant.

"Who are you?"

"Oh, I'm the one, your man has been spending his time with."

"If he's spending time with you, there's no way he's my man. Move on." I waved her away.

"That's what I said but he's still claiming you." She stood there.

"What the fuck you want?"

"I wanna fuck your man but he's giving me a hard time." I had to laugh at her ignorance. She was tryna get a rise outta me and since Ingrid and the girls are here, I'm not gonna give her the satisfaction.

"Why are you here?" Ingrid butted in.

"You must be Cason's woman."

"I'm not his woman and if you don't move the fuck on.-" She was about to go off but another woman walked over. She too, was pretty and her body was damn near spilling out her clothes.

"Who's this sis?" She explained who we were and the other chick looked us over.

"Damn, both of you are pregnant. No wonder, they out here tryna get their dicks wet. If I had to come home to a bunch of whales, I'd look elsewhere too."

"Not that your information is correct but how the hell do you know us?"

"Well, Cason has a picture of her and these two pretty girls on his phone." She pointed to Kiyah and Miracle.

"And Pierce showed me a photo of you last night, when we were together." I knew she was lying because he was at the hospital with Tiffany since she woke up and wouldn't leave until Cason came to get him. Last night, he called me half the fucking night and sent me tons of messages apologizing. His mom stepped out the room to call me too and said how stressed he was and had fallen asleep with Tiffany. She had to see me somewhere else.

"Ok, so now that we've been introduced, can we eat?"

"I guess but do me a favor and let Pierce go, so I can sample that big ass dick."

"If you didn't fuck him, how do you know if its big or not?"

"Oh, I walked in on him using the bathroom a few times." She had a smirk on her face.

"I guess you want me to do the same with Cason?" Ingrid asked.

"Cason and I are just friends for now. He won't allow me to get close to him at all. That nigga won't even kiss me. But it'll change soon. Don't you worry."

"Well, you better work harder if you want what he has in between his legs. Trust me, Cason is fucking amazing in the bedroom."

"Oh, I plan on finding out. Bye ladies." They finally walked off. We knew the reason they were being extra is to see our reaction. Neither of us, gave them the satisfaction.

"Bitch, are you crazy telling her how good Cason is?"

"Nope. If she's that confident, then I let her know its worth her time."

"Looks like I don't have to tell the other one shit about Pierce."

"Rebel, she didn't fuck him."

"Doesn't matter. They kissed and he was careless and allowed her to see his dick."

"I guess." The two of us sat there laughing and talking about our babies coming. I was now seven and a half months and she was going on five. I hope we both make it full term because these niggas are damn sure taking us through the ringer.

Roger

"And where are you going?" Odessa came in my room and plopped down on the bed.

"To meet up with Ingrid."

"That's stupid."

"Why is that?"

"You don't think she'll have Cason around to kill you?"

"She could but from what I hear they're not together."

She sat up quickly.

"Where did you get that information from?"

"I didn't get it from anywhere. I saw it."

I showed her a photo of Cason, his friend and two women sitting together at a club. They were laughing and having a good time. You wouldn't think they had women at home. One chick was all over the friend and Cason let the woman sit on his lap. I only saw them because some strippers were dancing in front of me and one mentioned it. It only made me nervous and I had both of them stand and walk with me out the back. Oh, but I sure took a photo and sent it to Ingrid. This was a few days ago and today she called to ask if we could meet up. I don't even care if its because of revenge or what. As long as, I could see her, its all that mattered to me.

I put my sneakers on and grabbed my things to leave. Odessa had a snarl on her face like she was mad. Its not my fault she tried to fuck him and his girl came. Granted, I called her but shit, my sister had him in there long enough to have done something. The crazy part is, my mom asked why didn't she fuck him instead and make him get her pregnant? She told her if it happened, not to mention it until it was too late so he couldn't force an abortion. So much for that theory because the nigga won't answer her calls or text messages.

"See you later son." My mom was in the kitchen cooking. I looked at her and she seemed to be happy. Here I am, still having bad days of my father dying in this very house and she's not having one issue.

I pulled out the back of the house in my mom's car because that's what I've been driving lately and went to the place she had me meet her. The hotel was big and the amount of people going in and out, appeared to have money. I pressed the elevator and rode it to the eleventh floor. I don't know why but there was something weird about having a room on an uneven floor. I walked down to the room and when she opened the door, I was blown away. Her stomach wasn't that big but you knew she was carrying. She stepped aside and let me in.

"How did that happen? I thought you couldn't get pregnant." The door locked and she came behind me.

"God works in mysterious ways." She smiled and showed me to the couch. I glanced around and the room was a suite. There was an upstairs and a small kitchen. She always did have good taste.

"I wanna thank you for sending me those photos and calling me to your house that night. It kept me from future heartbreaks." She sat next to me and I lifted her feet on my lap.

"Ingrid, you are a good woman and regardless of how I treated you, I never want you to hurt again." I massaged her feet and her head went back.

"That feels good Roger." The way she said it made my dick hard and so did the way she bit down on her lip.

"How does this feel?" I lifted the long dress up and let my fingers play with her clit through the panties.

"Sssss. Keep going." I put her legs on the floor, sat her up and got on my knees.

"Can I?" I had her panties by her ankles. She nodded and I took the chance to dive in.

"Shittttttt. Keep going." Her pussy was soaking my face up. I felt her legs lock around my head and she grinded her pussy all in my face.

"Yesssss." She let go and her breathing was really fast. I looked and once she calmed down, went back in to give her another one.

"You taste good Ingrid."

"Thanks. The bathroom is in there." She pointed and laid there. I walked in and the shit was immaculate. I wonder how much she paid for this damn room.

"You need help." She was standing up.

"What I needed help with, you handled it for me." She pulled my face to hers and started kissing me. She placed her hands in my jeans and had me strip.

"Did you miss me Roger?" She only had her birthday suit on. Her body was beautiful even with the pouch.

"I've always missed you." I let my pants hit the floor and then my boxers.

"I see." She pointed to my rock-hard dick.

"You want this pussy?" She had her index finger in her mouth. I didn't wanna fuck her pregnant but if she wants it, I'm not turning her down.

"Hell yea." I walked up on her and attacked her neck and let my fingers slide up and down her pussy.

"Lets take this outside." She led me on the balcony and the sight was amazing. You could see all of New York. If you looked down, everything looked small compared to being up here.

"I want you to fuck me out here."

"Ingrid, are you sure?" There were a few other balconies. Some people were smoking and others were either sitting or talking loud.

"I've never been fucked this high up." She had her back on the balcony and one of her legs were on the chair. Her pussy was exposed and I couldn't wait to be inside.

"Well, if its what you want." I surveyed the area and like I said, everyone was in their own world.

"Its what I want baby. Give it to me." I went closer.

"Did you really think, I'd let you fuck my woman?" My body froze. Ingrid had a smirk on her face.

"Put some fucking clothes on." He tossed Ingrid a robe.

"Cason, he ate my pussy really good." This bitch did not just tell him that. If I thought he may let me live; her saying that changed his mind.

"WHAT?"

"You heard me. I must say, he did an awesome job. Thanks Roger." She walked away and left him standing there with me.

"So, I guess you got what you wanted." He moved from behind me and passed my clothes.

"Actually, I didn't."

"The way I see it is, you tasted my girl again, your child was born and I haven't killed you yet. But you know what's crazy?" I buttoned my jeans.

"She called and told me you were here." I lifted my head.

"Yea. She said, if you kill this bastard, I may take you back. So, I flew over here because that woman owns my heart. If she asked me to blow up this world I would. Or if she asked me to kill your mother and sister, its done. She gets whatever she wants but you know what fucks me up?"

"Hold up. Did you hurt my mother and sister?"

"They were dead as soon as you left the house. See, I was on my way to kill you and everyone in there. Unfortunately, you had just left but don't worry, they suffered for you too." He had no sign of remorse in his voice.

"And what do you mean my baby was born? Rose didn't call me." He laughed like it was funny.

179

"Oh, she won't."

"Why not? That's my kid."

"Well, Rose died a while ago. Since you were hiding out, no one could tell you the kid was here. Now back to what fucks me up." He lit a blunt and stared at me.

"What fucks me up, is I allowed your sister to get me caught out there. Ingrid had and still has everything I need, yet; I wanted to kill you so bad, I messed up. Then, you get to taste her pussy one more time, which doesn't sit right with me." He blew smoke out.

"She wanted it." He nodded.

"She was sexually frustrated and again, its my fault. But now that she got her revenge because that's all it was, you won't ever see her again."

"You can't tell her what to do."

"Oh, like you did?" I shut right up. He moved closer to me.

"That pussy is mine and you better remember on your way down."

"My way down?"

"Goodbye Roger." I heard Ingrid say and my body flipped over the balcony. The entire way down, I saw my life flashing before me. There's no way, I'm surviving this. I closed my eyes and waited for impact.

Ingrid

"You think that shit is cute." I heard him yelling outside the bathroom door. After he pushed Roger over the balcony, I went to shower.

"INGRID!" I continued ignoring him. The glass door opened and he stood there with a snarl on his face. Again, I continued ignoring him and washed up.

"Oh you wanna ignore me." He reached in after I shut the water off and snatched me out. I had to hold on to the wall to keep from falling. I picked the towel up and began drying off. I was over his shit and he wasn't about to make me feel bad for my choice.

"Thanks for handling him but why are you still here?" He stared.

"How could you let him touch you?"

"The same way you let that bitch suck you off. How does it feel to know someone touched, what was supposed to be yours?"

"Ingrid." He reached out and I snatched away from him.

"Then something happened at your mothers and you snap on me, like I did it."

"Kiyah, may not be mine." I almost got whiplash turning so fast.

"What you say?" I had to be hearing him wrong.

"The night we made up and someone told me to go outside; Marsha was there." I sat on the bed to put lotion on.

"She handed me a note Desi wrote a long time ago and it described her infidelity."

"Cason, she could've written the letter herself."

"I thought the same thing." He leaned against the wall.

"After I snapped at you, I went to her grave. Some guy was there and come to find out, he in fact slept with her." I covered my mouth.

"Marsha found him somehow and told him about the letter and Kiyah. She offered to pay him 50k to take her if the test came back to say he's the father."

"Oh my God!"

183

"Lucky for me, he doesn't want any kids and told me he'd have a paper drawn up to keep me on her birth certificate and have the information stay hidden."

"How could he do that?"

"He's a lawyer." He handed me the letter and it stated, exactly what he told me.

"Have you taken the test?"

"A few days ago, a subpoena came in the mail and I had to bring her down with me." I stood in front of him.

"Cason, Kiyah is your daughter. I know people say kids resemble the person they've been with for a long time but she is your twin."

"I wanna believe it but its hard when there's doubt."

"Cason."

"Ingrid, I'm sorry for snapping on you and I know, I've said it before but I promise not to ever do it again. Marsha caught me off guard and I shouldn't have taken it out on you." I moved away and dropped my towel.

"Make love to me Cason." He smiled and placed his hand behind my head.

"I love you Ingrid with all that I have but I can't."

"Why not?"

"I know you were mad at me, I get it but you allowed him to touch you and right now, I can't handle it. To walk in this room and see you naked, only proved if you weren't pregnant, you'd most likely would've fucked him. Why would you do that to me?"

"You're right Cason. It was wrong but you're not going to make me feel bad for giving you a taste of your own medicine. I've been dealing with a lot and the moment you allowed Odessa to put you in a compromising position, only proved to me, had I not come you may have fucked her." I started putting my clothes on.

"Maybe, we aren't meant to be together. You did some foul shit and I returned the favor. People in love should never focus on revenge and that's exactly want I did but let me ask you something." I sat down and put my sneakers on.

"Are you acting this way because you're falling for the new chick you've been prancing around town?" I showed him a picture Roger sent me. He never said a word.

185

"You don't have to answer because your silence says a lot." I grabbed my things and headed for the door.

"You weren't ready for me and I blame myself for falling too fast for you. I craved the attention and love you offered and got lost in the fantasy. Goodbye Cason." I let the door shut and walked to the elevator. I still loved him but we're too far gone at this moment and space is what's best for both of us.

****

"Are you excited yet?" I asked Rebel as we got ready for her baby shower. It was at her house and the event planner set it up very nice. The crazy part is, she only invited her mom, my parents, Cason's mom and of course, Pierce's. A few of their cousins were coming and some of her mom's friends. When I say it was a small shower, it really was.

"Yea. Shit, this baby has been kicking my ass and I want my body back."

"I know the feeling. I had a few more months to go and cherished my pregnancy because I never thought it was possible.

"Girl please. Cason, is gonna get you pregnant right after this one." I hadn't told her what happened the night he killed Roger. She knew my plan and how he came to get rid of Roger but I never finished.

"Nah. We're done for good." She put the brush down and turned around.

"What happened?" I began telling her everything and broke down.

"Why didn't you tell me?"

"Rebel, you have a lotta shit going on too."

"I'm never too busy for you Ingrid. If you hurt, I'm the one who's supposed to cheer you up and vice versa."

"I know." I wiped my eyes.

"Let's get through your shower and go from there."

"Hell yea. You see all that food." She licked her lips with her greedy ass.

We finished getting ready and went downstairs. There was a knock at the door and she looked at me, as if I'd know who it was. I went passed her to the kitchen. I was hungry and like she said, it was tons of food. I walked back in the foyer area and saw Selina standing there with Syeed. What the hell were they doing there?

"Can we come in?" He asked.

"What the fuck you want Selina? Syeed, you can come in." I stood back eating my chicken wings.

"I came to apologize about my behavior. My insecurities had nothing to do with you. I was dealing with what happened years ago and thought I'd lose him the same way."

"What else?" Syeed said and she sucked her teeth.

"In a couple of months, I'll send you a place where we could meet up and finish the fight we had at the movies. Syeed and Pierce said, if our kids are going to be related, they don't want any issues at family functions and we need to get it over with." I busted out laughing.

"Is that all?"

"No. Here's a gift from us and again, I apologize." Rebel took the bag out her hand.

"Go to the car. I'll be right out." She stormed out.

"How did you end up back with her?"

"She had a lot of making up to do but once she did, I gave her another chance." He smirked.

"Spare me." He started laughing.

"I'm sorry for coming today but I knew, you'd be here for sure and she needed to do that. Also, when you taking that crazy ass nigga back?" He opened the front door.

"What?"

"That crazy nigga been bugging since you left him. Nigga's on the street don't even wanna speak when he's around because he snaps."

"What does that have to do with me?"

"Ummm, he told Selina he fucked up and did you similar, to the way I did. He couldn't get passed the way he saw you crying and hurting. Rebel, when a man is going through something, he may not act out like a female, so you won't be able to tell. He really does love you."

"Yea, well his actions showed otherwise."

"I'm not taking sides in this but remember you left out the job you did and whether, you slept with any of those niggas when you got with him, you still entertained them." She rolled her eyes.

"You went out with them. Called and text them and he caught one feeling you up in a hotel room. I'm not saying its revenge because he's working on something but you did it for the same reason." He kissed her on the cheek and closed the door. She looked at me and I walked away.

"What Ingrid?"

"I didn't say anything."

"You don't have to. Its all over your face."

"Rebel, you did what was best for you and as your friend, I'm here to support you."

"Hell no bitch. Do you agree?"

"Kinda and when I tried to tell you, you didn't wanna hear it."

I wasn't lying though. After she told me what went down, I tried to make her see it from someone on the outside looking in but she wasn't tryna hear it. I can see how it looked to her but once she mentioned he said, it wasn't what it looked like; I knew then it was more to the story. He asked me to talk to her and I did but she no longer wanted to dwell on it and I can't blame her. When Roger sent me the photo of him, Cason and those same bitches, it looked to be more than work.

"Whatever." She stormed off and left me in the living room watching television. She can act like a brat all she wants. I know she better bring her ass down here when these guests start coming. I ain't entertaining no one.

Cason

"Cason, why won't you let me kiss you?" Essence said and sat next to me on the couch. We were at the hotel she's been staying at.

"Essence we cool and all but kissing brings on emotions. We ain't no couple and I'm not sure what you're expecting outta this." I pointed between us.

"Neither is Pierce and Melanie but she's kissed him." I shook my head. I told his dumb ass not to let the bitch touch him. He didn't listen and it's the exact reason, Rebel left him.

"I have to go." I stood up and she tried her hardest to get my jeans down. After the shit with Odessa, I won't allow another woman to get me caught up. Ingrid, is the only woman I wanted and being we're not fucking with each other right now, I won't sleep with anyone.

"Where you going?"

"Yo, you not my girl."

"Obviously. Why you stuck on that big ass whale anyway?" I snapped my neck.

"Who you talking about?"

"The bitch on your phone. I ran into her at Chili's and she big as fuck. How you even fucking her?" I grabbed her by the head and slammed her on the ground.

"What did you say to her?"

"Nothing."

"Bitch, I will fucking kill you if you did anything to her."

"I swear, I didn't do anything." I could tell she was scared as hell. I no longer cared about messing up this job. Once she mentioned knowing anything about Ingrid, I had to draw the line.

"Be ready to fuck when I get back." Her head hit the floor.

"But you just said."

"I know what I said. Are we gonna have a problem?" She nodded her head no, like a good girl. Oh, I'm coming back but it won't be for what she wants.

I drove to Rebel's house to catch the ending of the baby shower and saw Pierce standing outside smoking. I knew he was nervous about going in. One… Rebel didn't tell him about it and two… he wasn't sure how he'd react. Rebel was giving him her ass to kiss and he was flipping on everyone. The shit was quite comical though. Niggas were literally scared to say anything to him.

"What up?"

"Shit. Man, I ain't going in."

"What?"

"I may snap her neck if she gets smart. Its best for me not to go in." He gave me a pound and got in his car. I thought about going in myself but then all the women would attack me and I'm good.

I drove to the house, put my car in the garage and went in to shower. Its been a long day and its going to be a long night. I stepped out, threw a pair of basketball shorts on and laid in the bed. I only wanted to take a nap. When I did wake up, she was standing there with her arms folded and a scowl on her face. She must've taken a shower because she had pajamas on.

"Why are you here?" I went in the bathroom to wash my face and get ready to leave.

"Cason, why are you here? I thought we decided.-" I shushed her with my lips.

"We didn't decide anything. You wanted me to make love to you and I said no. You took it to another level and left." I removed the pajamas and made her get on the bed.

"No Cason." I spread her ass cheeks open and put my face in.

"Oh my gawdddd. Fuckkkkkkk!"

"Let it go Ingrid." I stuck a finger in her ass and the other in her pussy. Her body was shaking.

"Beautiful." I smacked her ass.

"Turn over." She did what I asked.

"You wanted me to make love to you." She nodded.

"Its exactly what I'm gonna do." She didn't say a word and the two of us were moaning out each other's name. Her stomach got in the way a little but it didn't bother me, one bit.

She fell asleep in my arms and a nigga stayed all night. I'll deal with the other bitch tomorrow. I have to make sure my home front is good.

****

"Daddy!" I opened my eyes and Kiyah was jumping on the bed.

"Where's Ingrid?"

"Cooking." I smiled and stopped her from jumping.

"Good because I'm hungry. What about you?" I lifted her upside down and took her in the bathroom.

"Did you brush your teeth?"

"No."

"Go get your toothbrush and come brush them with daddy." She ran out the room and while she did, I locked the bathroom door to use it. I washed my hands and heard her little knock.

"I'm ready." I sat her on the sink and applied toothpaste to both of our brushes.

"Like this daddy." She put her toothbrush up and had me copying the way she did it.

"Now do your tongue."

"I hate that."

"Too bad." She did it and gagged twice. I had to tell her not to go as far. No wonder she hated it.

After we finished and washed our faces, we went downstairs. Miracle was in the walker tearing shit up, as usual. I kissed her forehead and went in the kitchen. Kiyah was asking for orange juice. I looked around and Ingrid was making a little of everything. Pancakes, eggs, bacon, toast, home fries, and there was cut up fruit on the counter. I asked who was all the food for and she said, some people were coming over.

"I thought you were cooking for me." I wrapped my arms around her.

"You ate last night and very well, I may add."

"I would've ate again this morning if you didn't get outta bed." I turned her around.

"I'm sorry for hurting you Ingrid."

"Why did you hurt her daddy?" Kiyah's nosy ass asked.

"It was an accident."

"Did you give her a band aid for it?"

"She got a big band aid last night for it."

"CASON!" She smacked me on the arm.

"You did."

"Whatever. Your mom and the others will be here shortly. Can you put some clothes on?"

"What they coming for?"

"Cason, we have brunch every week at someone's house."

"I didn't know that." I grabbed a piece of bacon.

"Its because you were in your own world." She went to walk away.

"I'm not going anywhere. I'm back and we're gonna be together like we were before."

"I hope so." I made her look at me.

"We are."

"Oh Cason." She handed me an envelope and the look on her face told me it's the one, I don't want. She put her hand on mine.

"Kiyah is your daughter, regardless; of what this paper says. Remember that."

"Open it."

"Huh?" I handed it to her.

"Open it. I can't."

"Cason, the results won't change no matter who opens it."

"I know but you're my lucky charm."

She put the fork down, wiped her hands on the apron and picked the envelope back up. As she tore it open, all I could think of was the day Desi delivered her. It was the happy moment in my life. I held her and new from then on, promised I'd protect her with my life. Each day that has gone by since Marsha told me that shit, its been fucking torture. The guy told me he didn't want kids but who knows if that will change in the future? Will he be able to come back and claim her? I had so many thoughts running through my head.

"Cason, you know once I read this, it won't change a thing."

"Ingrid, what does it say? Give me the truth, I can handle it." She went to speak.

"WAIT! Don't tell me."

"Baby, if I don't tell you, all you're gonna do is wonder, so why not find out?"

"I'm nervous."

"Why?" She sat across from me.

"Is my love going to change for her? Will I look at her different? What if?-"

"Cason, you love her too much for any of that to happen."

"Fine! Give me the results." She looked down at the paper and then at me.

"I fucking knew it. I'm gonna kill him so he can't try and take her later in life." I was pacing the kitchen floor. Kiyah came in and Ingrid lifted her up. I had to yell at her. She was too big, for her to be carrying her.

"Cason, she's yours." It was like the earth stood still. I snatched the paper out her hand. My eyes scanned it to reach the results. The test was 99.99999% mine.

"I love you so much Kiyah."

"Daddy! Put me down." I had her up in the air, swinging around.

"Cason, she just drank all that juice. She's gonna.-" Ingrid didn't get to finish because Kiyah literally threw up the juice. She started crying and reached out for my girl. The love those two had for one another only verified her being my wife. No other woman would be in Kiyah's life but Ingrid and I mean it.

"I'm happy for you baby." She was cleaning Kiyah up in the bathroom. I had Miracle in my arms drinking a bottle.

"Thank you for everything Ingrid."

"I didn't do anything."

"You did more than enough." I told her to look at me.

"You took on a man with a lotta baggage and stuck around though it all. You never folded and made me see I couldn't play with your heart. I swear, you're the only woman I want in my life or around my kids. Will you marry me?" Her eyes popped open. I put Miracle on the floor and got on my knees in front of her. Kiyah hopped on my back.

"I don't have a ring yet and I know this is sudden but baby, I don't wanna waste any more time trying to figure out when to ask. Every day, you show me why you should be the wife."

"CASON!" She put her index finger on my lips.

"I'm nervous ma. I've never asked a woman to marry me." I wanted to marry Desi and said she was going to be my wife but never got around to asking. I didn't wanna make the same mistake and miss out.

"Yes, I'll marry you." She placed her lips on mine and had the girls not been there, we definitely would've done a lot more.

"I fucking love you Ingrid and you'll have a ring before the end of the day." She placed her hand on my face.

"Cason, take your time. I'm not going anywhere. Plus, my ring better be big as Rebel's, if not bigger, so make sure you do a good job at choosing one. K!" She patted my face and picked our daughter up.

"Bigger? What about not needing a big ring?" I asked her a few months back what she thought about marriage and what kind of ring would she like. She told me, the size of the ring didn't matter.

"That was before you kept messing up." She smiled and left me and Kiyah standing there. That woman is a mess but I love her.

Pierce

"How the hell you propose with no ring? That's some ghetto shit."

"I was happy to find out Kiyah was mine and it just came out." Everyone in the family was happy to find out she was his. It would've taken a toll on him and most likely my aunt and uncle, who loved the shit outta their grandkids. I'm not saying they would love her less but its different when you find out something you've known for the past few years, is no longer yours.

"I planned on asking her when this shit with these bitches were over but fuck it."

"Yea, I'm over these ho's."

"That reminds me. Why you kissing the bitch? We were supposed to get close and keep it moving."

"It happened one time and by accident."

"Accident?"

"I was in the bathroom and the bitch came in to see my dick." He gave me a crazy look.

"Exactly. I washed my hands and she was sitting on the sink. She grabbed my shirt and put her lips on mine. I should've pulled back but went with it. I ain't gonna lie; she did get my dick hard. That's when I knew, I fucked up."

"Ya think."

"Hell yea. I messed up and I ain't been sleeping good at all, without my girl."

"Go get her."

"Soon as we get these bitches." I parked at the hotel, we had the chicks meet us at.

We knew exactly who Melanie and Essence were. Cason and I, went to the club for that reason. Sway, thought we didn't know after he found out about Rebel being my girl, he sent some chicks up to try and get us. I can admit how bad they were and even though I fucked up, Reb is still the only one for me. That's why I'm taking it so hard because she won't fuck with me. Since we met, we've woken up together, spoke on the phone all day, every day and spent every chance we could together. Hell yea, a nigga was spoiled.

The day she caught me texting Melanie, I should've come out and told her everything, but Rebel is just like me and doesn't listen. She for sure, would've tried to get at Sway or the women. She was right about me entertaining the chick too much and I swear it wasn't for revenge. Sway, didn't know but we had someone watching his wife, hoping she would meet up with him. Unfortunately, she did the night something happened to my daughter. I was so messed up, I couldn't even function to send anyone. I told them to fall back and we'd get him later.

These bitches come around and at first, they were tight lipped. After a few times meeting up with them and slipping shit in their drinks, we knew the entire plan. Sway, was mad about Rebel being my girl and having a baby by me. Supposedly, he was still in love with her and assumed she'd come back.

What I wanna know is why he thought that, knowing he had a wife at home? I swear, men these days make it hard for real niggas. I parked in the lot and we both got out. My phone rang and shockingly it was Rebel. I sent it to voicemail because I needed no distractions for what I'm about to do. She called two more times, when we were on the floor and about to go in the room.

"Yo!"

"Nigga, get your punk ass down to the hospital."

"For what Reb? I'm busy and.-"

"I'm in fucking labor, you asshole. I swear, if I have this baby before you get here, I won't speak to you ever again." The phone hung up.

"We have to take a rain check."

"Nah. You go ahead. I got this."

"You sure?"

"Yea man. I'm over this shit and Ingrid just took me back. I refuse to sleep without her again."

"I feel ya."

"Hurry up and go."

"Shit, I'm nervous."

"You should be. Its damn sure a sight to see." He don't know how much worse he made it.

"Maybe, I should wait."

"Ok but I'm not having your back when she asks why you didn't make it." He knocked on the door to the hotel room. Melanie opened it and both women stood there naked. Cason told them we were going to switch up throughout the night.

"Hey baby." Essence tried to kiss him.

PHEW! Her body dropped and Melanie started screaming. I grabbed her by the hair and heard my cousin on the phone getting people to come clean this mess.

"When is he coming?"

"Please don't kill me."

"When is he coming?" My phone started ringing again. I looked down and it was my mother. I had to hurry up.

"He'll be here next week."

"Where he staying?" She gave me all the information I needed and met her fate as well. I couldn't let her live. I gave Cason a pound and ran out the room and down the steps.

"Yea ma."

"Where the fuck you at?"

"I'm coming. Tell her she better not fucking deliver until I get there."

"Boy, shut up." She hung the phone up laughing.

****

"We need you to push ma'am." The doctor said to Rebel, who was being difficult. I been here for three hours waiting on her to deliver. When I first got here, she was only five centimeters and now she's ten.

"I am pushing but this kid won't come out." I busted out laughing.

"Why you laughing? I bet your ass don't get no pussy for a very long time." She wiped the smile right off my face.

"I bet your ass won't suck my dick either." I whispered in her ear. Now that she's become a pro at doing it, sometimes its all she wanted to do.

"You get on my nerves."

"But yo as love me." She rolled her eyes and laid her head back. I placed a kiss on her lips and she squeezed my hand tighter.

"There's the head." I ran to the other end of the bed and sure shit, you could see the top of my kids' head.

"Pierce, come hold my hand."

"Hell no. You squeeze too tight and I wanna see my little nigga coming out." We didn't know the sex of the baby but I wanted a boy.

"Ahhhhhh." She screamed and the head popped out. The doctor used this tube looking thing in my kids' nose and mouth. The scream was loud as hell.

"One more push and your baby will be out."

"Pierce?"

"What man. Hurry up so I can see if I got a son or daughter." She sucked her teeth.

"Fuck this." I pulled my phone out and started recording. I'm gonna have to watch this shit again. Rebel pushed one more time. The baby came out and so did blood and clear shit.

"Yuk!"

"Mommy and daddy, you have a baby boy."

"YES!" I shouted and saw her eyes roll. I walked over to the nurse weighing him and watched. She cleaned him off, took his footprints, handprints, did a few other things and turned around to hand him to me. I placed my phone in my pocket and took him from her.

"Damn, Pierce Jr. You scream loud as hell." I walked over to let Reb see him. The doctor had her pushing the afterbirth or some shit out.

"Ma, why you crying?" Both of our moms were in there.

"Because we missed Tiffany's birth. Thanks for letting me be here Rebel." She kissed her forehead.

"Ummm, I let y'all be here." All three of them sucked their teeth.

"Whatever."

"You wanna hold him Reb?"

"Not right now Pierce. Let me sleep for a few." I glanced over at the doctor.

"After a woman gives birth, she's always tired. The pushing and straining, really wears their body out. Its normal." I nodded and watched her close her eyes.

"Pierce, you better make it right." Her mom said, kissed Rebel and my son and left. She told me to tell her, she'd be back in the morning.

"At least, I know she'll still be around the family even if she doesn't take you back." I gave my mother a fake smile.

"I'll see you tomorrow and Tiffany needs new sneakers."

"For what? Reb, just got her some two weeks ago."

"Boy, she's starting preschool in a few weeks and she wants a new pair for every day of the first week."

"Hell no. She bugging. Who in the hell would tell her, she needed a different pair, each day?" She pointed to Rebel and I had to laugh. My girl had fucking shoes, purses and clothes for days. I sometimes catch her and Tiffany playing dress up and the high heels look crazy on my daughter; yet, sexy as fuck on my girl. I looked over at her and smiled. Yea, I had to make shit right with her.

Rebel

"Pierce?" I nudged him a little to wake up. Today, the doctor was discharging me and my son. I wanted to get cleaned up so when he came, we could leave right away. I sent him to the house yesterday to get us some clothes. I had a bag packed for the baby and forgot to put my own shit in it.

"Pierce, get up." He opened his eyes and looked on his chest. My son was knocked out. Any time I tried to take him, Pierce had a fit. Talking about he not gonna be a momma's boy. The only time he let me hold him, is to breastfeed and his ass got mad off that. Saying, he's the only one who should be sucking on them.

"Come help me in the bathroom."

"Why you ain't call the nurse?" He stood, put our son in the crib, changed his diaper and placed the binky in his mouth.

"You know what? It is a male nurse on duty. Let me get him in here to help me wash."

214

"And I'll fuck you up too." He stretched and came towards me.

"Come on before I forget about you bleeding and fuck you in the ass."

"God, why did you send me this man?"

"That's because he knew this sexy, big dick nigga, would have you strung out."

I shook my head and made him wait until I cleaned my pussy. I'm only allowed to squirt down there right now. I needed him to help me stand to take a ho bath. He came in and watched me. After I finished, he lifted my leg in the sweats and put my socks on. I started brushing my teeth and he stood behind me. I felt his lips on my neck and his hands were roaming my body. I glanced in the mirror and we looked good together.

"I'm sorry ma."

"Me too." I had to apologize for lashing out on him too. Syeed, made a good point about us being in the same line of work. I didn't wanna see it for what it, was when it came to him and automatically claimed him to be cheating. Don't get me wrong, he had no business kissing or even entertaining her while we were together but I get it.

"You coming home?" He turned me around to face him.

"If you want me there." I let my hands go behind his neck.

"I want my son there and I know you come as a package deal, sooooo."

"Don't play with me." I let my hands go in his jeans to massage his dick.

"Reb, you know I can't have none. Stop playing."

"Oh, you don't want me to touch you?" I undid his jeans and let them drop, along with his boxers.

"Dude, your dick is huge." He started laughing.

"Yea but you know that because you love sucking and riding it."

"That, I do." I jerked him slowly and began kissing him.

"It feels good ma but I'm gonna cum fast." I smiled.

"Then get it out the way so when I get you home and suck your soul out, it won't be as fast." I stroked him faster and even let my sweats down a little so the tip was on the top of my pussy.

"Shitttttt." He yanked me by the hair and came hard. He hopped in the shower and I went in the room after hearing my son cry. I thought, I was bugging when this bitch leaned in to get my son.

"ARE YOU FUCKING CRAZY?" I punched her on the side of the face.

"Reb, you good?" I heard Pierce yelling from the bathroom. I couldn't answer because I was banging this bitch head into the wall.

"Yooooo. Calm down." I heard Cason and felt him lifting me up. My son stopped crying and I looked over to see Ingrid holding him.

"Why is this bitch here? She was trying to pick my son up." Pierce came running out the bathroom in a pair of jeans and his upper body was still wet. He must've heard me and rushed to throw something on.

"You ok? My son good?" He had me against the wall and turned his head to see where he was.

"Shayla was here, tryna take our son out the crib. How did she know and if she's back we have to get Tiffany?"

"Where she go?"

"She ran, after Cason pulled me off her."

"Babe, take the baby for a minute." Ingrid passed him to Cason and came over to me.

"Pierce, let her clean up." She pointed to my pants and I had blood all over them.

"Shit! You hurt." I shook my head no and Ingrid came in with me.

"I know you shouldn't take a shower but that's too much blood to clean off with a rag. Be careful in there, Rebel." She started the shower and stepped out. I heard the door close and the shower curtain opened. He took his jeans off and got in with me; blood and all.

"I'm gonna get her Reb."

"What if he didn't cry? What if she took him?"

"Look at me." I stared up at him.

"She won't get you, my son or my daughter. Let's get cleaned up and go home." I nodded.

I washed up very carefully and watched the blood go down the drain. He wasn't disgusted and even stayed to wash my back. Once we finished, he wrapped a towel around himself, handed me clean panties and two pads. I had him bring me the always overnights because the hospital pads were humungous and I wasn't walking out wearing one. I cleaned the bathroom up and he finished getting dressed. I couldn't wait to get outta here.

****

"You're next." I told Ingrid. We were at her house with the kids. Its been two weeks since I delivered and the only reason I'm here, is because Pierce's mom is at my house and told me to get some fresh air. Her and my mom, were a big help with the kids.

"Did it hurt really bad?"

"I had an epidural so I only felt a small amount of pressure but its hard to push."

"What you mean?"

"With the epidural, I couldn't really feel the contractions so when he told me to push, I felt I was but he kept saying I wasn't."

"Maybe, I shouldn't get one."

"Oh, you'll want it."

"But I thought you didn't really feel it."

"Girl, they make you wait until you're almost ten centimeters before they give it. I felt a lot before, which is why I begged for one."

"Great!"

"Don't be nervous. Just think, about the life you're about to bring in this world."

"I think Cason is more excited than I am." She smiled. It was good to see them back together.

"That nigga excited you took him back."

"Whatever."

"I'm serious. Pierce told me, about the bullshit Marsha pulled with Kiyah and how you were the one who opened the envelope. Ingrid, you are the only person he wanted to be there when he found out. If not, he would've taken it out the house."

"I guess."

"Don't sell yourself short. He's in love with you and despite his stupidity, he knows you won't play those cheating games. Kiyah's mom may have but he knows you won't."

"Can you believe his precious Desi, cheated?"

"Bitchhhhhhh, I know. I bet its why he snapped."

"It is." We turned around and he was standing there smiling at Ingrid.

"I never thought she would dip out but it is, what it is. If she were alive, I would've probably killed her." He said it calmly, which made me look at Ingrid. He went in the kitchen.

"We really have some crazy ass niggas."

"I have to agree."

"INGRID! What's this?" She waddled over to him.

"What?"

"This." He pulled her in for a kiss and moved her hand down.

"I'm out. You couldn't wait until I left."

"I know you're not talking Rebel. Shit, had my cousin moaning loud as hell, knowing I was in the living room waiting." I gave him the finger. The other day, he came by and Pierce was in the shower. I told him Cason was waiting for him and he pulled me in with him. We couldn't have sex yet, so he played around my clit and made me cum. All I did, was get on my knees and return the favor. How the hell was I supposed to know, he'd get a little loud?

"I'll see you later Ingrid and Tiffany is getting dropped off here."

"For what?" Cason yelled.

"Babe, they're having a sleep over. Kiyah asked you yesterday and you said yea.

"Man, they together too much."

"They're related and what you think is gonna happen when your niece gets older?" I referred to Selina's baby. She had a daughter a month ago and hell yea, I'm waiting on that call to tag her ass. We'll never be friends but at least that part will be outta the way.

"Whatever. That reminds me. Lil Syeed has a basketball game tomorrow." He was on the AAU team and the coach loved him. I have to say, he was pretty good too. Him and Pierce wanted to spend more time with him but he traveled a lot with the team and barley got to see him. If there was a game, they'd make sure to make it and cause all types of scenes. If the referee called a foul on Syeed, it would be a fucking mess. A few times, they almost got kicked out.

"I'll see you later." I closed the door and drove home. When I got there, Pierce was there and his mom's car wasn't.

"What up?" Tiffany was on his lap and Junior was in the swing. I admired how he bonded with his daughter. Its crazy how her mother kept her away and now Tiffany hated to be away from us. If she wasn't with Kiyah or his mom, she'd be right under us. I took a seat next to them and he grabbed my hand.

"What's wrong?"

"Nothing." He slid my ring back on.

"Who said, I was still marrying you?"

"I did and I wish you would take it off again. Do you know how much that motherfucker cost?"

"No, how much?"

223

"A whole fucking lot and you taking it off, like its your money."

"It was."

"No the hell it wasn't."

"What's yours is mine, so I basically bought this." He was laughing so hard he had to hold his stomach.

"Oh, its not 50/50?"

"You got that Reb. Just make sure you don't take it off again."

"Yea Rebby. Daddy said, I can't take mine off either." I looked and he brought her a small gold ring.

"And you say I spoil her." He waved me off and laid his head on my lap. Tiffany laid at the other end of the couch. This is my family and I couldn't wait to become Mrs. Pierce Hill.

Ingrid

"Good morning." I said to the woman when she opened the door.

"Can I help you?"

"My name is Ingrid and.-" She covered her mouth.

"I guess you know who I am."

"Yes, come in." She opened the door and let me walk in. I had Kiyah with me because we were only stopping here for a minute. She had dance lessons in an hour.

"Do you want something to drink?"

"No, I'll just take a few minutes of your time." She offered me a seat on the couch. Her house was nice and I noticed all the baby things.

"Let me start off by apologizing for all the wrong things my daughter Rose did to you. I told her a hundred times to leave you alone. Its like she was obsessed with destroying you, in order to keep a man who couldn't even save her." I noticed her eyes getting glassy.

"Unfortunately, we can't help who we love and we all know, love makes people do crazy things." She nodded and Kiyah asked if she could turn cartoons on for her.

"I stopped by because Roger left a life insurance policy in my name for half a million dollars and since you have his kid, its only right to give you the money."

"No offense but why did he leave it to you?"

"I'm not offended and I ask myself the same question. I believe it was guilt money for what he put me through. I figured he would change it but he didn't." I heard a baby cry and she excused herself. She returned with an exact replica of Roger.

"WOW!"

"I have no idea who he looks like."

"You never met Roger?"

"No. Rose knew, I didn't approve of her being a side chick and never brought him by."

"I don't have any photos of him but just know, he looks exactly like him."

"I figured that because he looks nothing like Rose."

"Well, I just wanted to give you this." The insurance company sent me a check. I cashed it and wrote this one for her.

"Thank you and again, I'm sorry she put you through that."

"I appreciate the apology and all she did is place Cason and my stepdaughter in my life."

"This is his daughter?"

"Yes."

"I haven't seen her since she was a baby. I was always working and kept saying I'd go see her and never made it. Then once her mom passed, I stayed away."

"From what I hear, he took it very hard."

"I bet. They were together for a long time. But at least she has you and I can tell how much you love her and vice versa." Kiyah was sitting close to me and hadn't moved. Usually she's on my lap but my stomach is too big.

"Yup. That's my munchkin." I stood up to leave.

"Thanks for stopping by and I'm glad you're happy and moving on with your life."

"I am. It was nice meeting you."

"You too." She hugged me and Kiyah. We walked to the car and she got in the car seat. Kiyah was four now and knew how to put her own seatbelt on and everything. I started the car and drove to our next spot. My life was finally perfect.

****

"I can't wait until you have my baby." Cason was standing behind me as we watched Kiyah get her things together. Her dance class was over and we were supposed to go out to eat.

"Are you happy with me?" I asked.

"Hell fucking yea." He made me look at him and got down on one knee. The music stopped and everyone looked over at us.

"Ingrid, you are the only woman I wanna be with. I know, you told me yes but I had no ring, which showed me, it really is about my love and not my money. You accepted my daughter before you even thought about being with me and that too, tells me a lot. You have two of my daughters and are about to bless me with another baby. I love you so much and I wanna be the only man in your life forever." He pulled a box out his pocket and opened it. The ring was pink and gigantic.

"Look up." I did what he asked and there stood some of Kiyah's friends holding up big cards with the words, *Will you marry me?*

"Cason?" My parents and his family were standing there recording and taking pictures. I had no clue anyone was even here.

"Marry my daddy, Ingie." She handed me a bouquet of roses and kissed my cheek.

"Well?"

"Yes Cason. I'll be your forever." He slid the ring on my finger and everyone started clapping. He stood up and kissed me.

"Kiss me daddy." He placed one on her cheek and Miracle who was in the stroller, wanted him to pick her up.

"I love you baby." He turned me to face him.

"I love you too and we're gonna be married after we leave."

"SAY WHAT NOW!" I looked at my clothes and they were not wedding material.

"You heard me."

"No, Cason. I wanna big wedding and.-"

"You can have one later but my baby will have married parents." I folded my arms.

"Can y'all get Kiyah?"

"Cason, I'm not marrying you today." I handed Miracle to my mom and grabbed Ingrid's hand.

"Get in the truck."

"No."

"Fine!" He lifted me up and put me inside. How the hell he lifted me and the baby in my stomach is beyond me. But then again, he is strong as hell. We drove for about ten minutes and stopped in front of some small church.

"Get out." I sat there and called Rebel."

"Bitch, you better not walk down the aisle until I get there."

"I'm not getting married today. This is not the way I wanted it."

"Bye Rebel." He hung the phone up and pulled me out the truck.

"You can stand there all you want but if you're not inside that motherfucking church in ten minutes, I promise to carry you." I sucked my teeth and sat on the bench. I noticed everyone pulling up and none of them came over to me. They waved and went in the church.

"So, you just gonna sit out here while everyone else is inside?" I heard Cason yelling on his way out. I didn't move.

"I told you what would happen." He lifted me up and carried me inside.

"Get off me. I said, I didn't wanna get married like this. I'm not gonna say I do. Put me down." I was hitting him in the back.

"If you go into early labor and don't have my last name before you deliver, that's your ass."

"Cason, there's no decorations or.-" He turned me around and the church definitely was set up. It wasn't perfect but enough for me to appreciate it.

"Now walk down this damn aisle when the music plays." My father grabbed my hand.

"Cason."

"Ingrid, you better walk down the damn aisle." He left me standing there.

"I guess he told you."

"DADDY!"

"Ingrid. Stop being a brat. He knows you want a huge wedding but he also wants you to be his wife before the baby is born. The way I see it is, you're compromising."

"How is that when he's making me?"

"Because you're gonna be his wife and when the baby is born, you'll get the wedding you want."

"But.-"

"But nothing. That man loves you and what you need to do is walk down this aisle before he comes back to get you."

"You're supposed to be on my side."

"I am. Don't you see me walking with you?"

"Very funny." The music stopped when we got there and Cason took my hand in his. This isn't the wedding of my dreams but I guess, its enough for now. He better know, I'm

sparing no expense for my dream one.

Cason

After the ceremony, I took Ingrid to the Waldorf Astoria to celebrate our honeymoon. She wasn't allowed to fly until the baby was born but she loved it here. I don't know how many times we had sex over the last couple of days but I needed to get as much as I could before she delivered.

"You got everything?" I asked as she took her time coming to the door.

"Yea. Can we come back here?"

"Anytime you want." I kissed her lips and walked out hand in hand, with my wife. It sounded crazy but I wouldn't change a thing. I placed our bags in the trunk and answered my phone.

"Yo!"

"Mr. Hill."

"Yea, who this?"

"Hi. We met at the cemetery." This is my first time speaking to him, since that night. Everything went through my lawyer.

"What up?"

"I'm calling because as you know, your daughter is indeed yours. However; the woman has not stopped contacting me."

"What you mean?"

"Well, I told her the child is yours and she's been hounding me, to tell the judge some nonsense about the test being altered. I don't know what's going on but she is trying extremely hard to get the little girl."

"Thanks for letting me know and I'll handle that."

"Ok. Take care." He ended the call and Ingrid looked at me.

"Marsha, still on her shit."

"Why?"

"She wants the lawyer to say the test was altered so she can get Kiyah."

"Handle her Cason and make sure she doesn't return." I smirked at her asking me to kill her.

"Look at you giving me orders to end someone's life."

"If it affects my family, then you damn right."

"Gimmie a kiss." We were sitting at a light.

"How about I give you this instead." She unzipped my jeans and topped me off. I sat right there at the light enjoying it, until a horn blew. I pulled over on a deserted street and let her finish. The married life ain't as bad as people make it.

****

"Its about time. You should've killed her ass a long time ago." Pierce was in the passenger seat rolling a blunt.

"I tried to give her the benefit of the doubt but look where it got me? I almost lost my daughter and snapped on my girl and she left me. Before she can cause any more problems, I'm getting rid of her. Plus, Ingrid wants her outta here. And a happy wife makes a happy life."

"Yea, I know."

"When you and Rebel getting married?"

"She talking about next week and have a big one later."
I started laughing.

"Man, you did that shit." I didn't deny it.

We drove to this bitch house, sat outside and finished the blunt before going in. I knew she was home because miserable people don't leave the house much. Once he tossed the roach, we stepped out and I knocked on the door. Because she took so long opening it, I kicked it open. I couldn't believe my damn eyes. She tried to hurry and cover herself but it was too late.

"Bitch, you get high and fucking niggas on the couch?"

"Don't worry about my business and why are you here?"

"What you mean don't worry? You tried hard as hell to get my daughter and this is the shit you would've brought her into."

"What do you want?" Whoever the guy was looked half dead. I guess the drugs had him gone.

"To end this nonsense, you have going on."

"You know Kiyah will be with me soon enough. I got the lawyer to say the test was altered. You don't deserve my granddaughter." She smiled. She was lying through her yellow ass teeth.

"What's your issue with me?"

"Ever since you cheated on my daughter, I have never liked you. Desi told me all about the guy she cheated with and how Kiyah may not be yours. I didn't have proof at the first court date but when I found that letter, God answered my prayers."

"And how is that?"

"Because even though she turned out to be yours, I saw how much it hurt you. Shit, I sat in my car watching you snap on the bitch, you claimed to love. I loved seeing you hurt. And I'm the one who made sure the guy was at the cemetery, that night. I knew you'd go there after hearing the news and you did. Boy oh boy, the joy I received as I looked at your face. Say what you want and kill me but to see you hurting, is all I ever wanted. Now if you'll excuse me, I wanna finish getting high and fucking."

"Too bad!"

PHEW! PHEW! I put a bullet in her and the guy's head.

To hear she got joy outta hurting me didn't bother me at all. I knew the type of woman she was. I wasn't even mad, she sent the guy to Desi's grave. It was an eye opener for me. Desi, wasn't as perfect as I thought and it proves we all have secrets. The only difference is, Desi literally took hers to the grave and had her mom not found the letter, I still wouldn't know. I made my normal call for a mess to be cleaned up and took my ass home to my wife.

Pierce

"Damn baby. Your snap back body is the shit." I let my hands go all over her body. She had on all black and the outfit showed every curve. Her chest was still bigger than normal from breastfeeding my son.

"Pierce, we're on a schedule. Come on." She opened the bedroom door.

"Reb, I think you should change. My dick hard."

"Baby, your dick is always hard for me."

"That is true." She pecked me on the lips and both of us kissed the girls' goodbye. Her mom was watching them, while we went outta town. Everyone was at the house waiting for us to go.

Sway was in town and tonight is the best time to hit. He was throwing a party at a mansion and we weren't invited. Now, Cason told him previously never to enter someone's backyard without informing them. He must've forgot because he damn sure slipped in, thinking no one knew.

"Be careful, you two." My mom said and kissed her boyfriend.

Where we were going, he refused to let us go without him. Hell, Cason's pops, was rolling with us too. Because we were going in blind, the OG's wasn't tryna hear us go in with our regular team. They trusted them but when their mind is set, its no changing it. I guess, that's why Cason and I are the same, when it comes to that.

"Rebel, please be careful." Ingrid looked like she was about to cry.

"I'm going to be fine Ingrid. This is what I do." She looked at me.

"Well did. Plus, my fiancé, your husband, his pops and Pierce's pops, will be there. You know Sam and Jeff are going, too. There will be a bunch of people there." She always referred to Charles as my pops. Sometimes I'd call him that myself.

"Ok. I'll see you later." They hugged and all of us headed out the door. MJ, his brother Alex and a few others were just pulling up. When I say we were ready for this nigga, we really were.

"You're gonna be fine. She's as thorough as you." I told Rebel and pointed to Cecily, who was on our team too. When Rose died, we gave her the position and she hasn't let us down yet. She's actually the reason we're gonna get this punk ass nigga.

See, Cecily knew who Sway was and once we heard he was back in town a while back, we sent her to the places he frequented. Cecily, is a bad chick and one look at her and Sway was game. Anyway, he asked her if she knew us and she said not really and it was on from there. He's been conspiring with her to get us. Yesterday, he asked if she knew Rebel and she told him yes. He went on about her being his long-lost cousin and asked if she could find and bring her to him, which is how we got to this point. I wasn't comfortable with her doing anything but she fucked that right outta me.

We parked down the street from the house he was throwing a party at. Rebel, already told us about the massive amount of security he has. MJ, had been doing research on him too and found out about the wife. Evidently, she comes from money because her father used to be a kingpin and he had people on standby for Sway, if he ever needed help. For some reason, they were in town too.

"I'll be by your side, the whole time." Cecily told her when she got out. Rebel wasn't scared but I could definitely tell she was nervous.

"Pierce, don't let anything happen to me, when you get inside." I pulled her close.

"You can back out if you want Reb. Cecily, can do this."

"I know you just had a baby and I would be worried too." Cecily told her.

"No, I'm ok." She fixed her clothes.

"Here." MJ passed her some type of button and told her to put it on her belt.

"This will let us see what's going on inside. If for some reason you feel shit is about to get outta hand, press it and we'll come right in." She put it on and you couldn't tell it was anything but what belonged on it.

"Yo, Can you see?" He yelled out to someone. The person peeked out the truck and put his thumb up.

"Here Cecily. Because you have on a dress, attach it to your clutch." She too did the same. We got some high-tech shit but damn.

"Love you baby." She pecked my lips.

"Thanks MJ." Rebel gave him a hug and the two of them got back in the car.

"She'll be fine. I have niggas in there too." I turned to him.

"What? Shit, Cason may be my blood cousin, but you're his family. Therefore; his family is mine as well. And Morgan would kill me if anything happened to her and I could've stopped it."

"Thanks, cuz."

"Anytime. Now, let's get ready to go in." I walked to the truck with Cason and he was on the phone with Ingrid through the Bluetooth. You could hear her asking a bunch of questions.

"She's gonna be fine Ingrid. We'll be home soon."

"Pierce, I'm gonna kick your ass if anything happens to her."

"Bye Ingrid." Cason disconnected the Bluetooth and we all sat there waiting.

"You're gonna be fine." Cecily kept saying but it didn't feel like it. I haven't been in this type of situation in a very long time. Its feels like my first job.

"Ok. I'm ready." We stepped out and one of the guys looked us up and down before opening the door. He must've gotten new security because his guys knew who I was.

We walked in without being searched, which is a crazy because Sway had never allowed anyone in with weapons. As we stepped through the house, I noticed the normal going on. Niggas fucking women any and everywhere. Some were playing a video game, on their phone and playing cards. One person caught my eye and I had Cecily follow me upstairs to where they went. I opened the door and she turned around with the look of terror on her face.

"What are you doing here?"

"The question is, what are you doing here?"

"This is my man's house." Cecily and I both started laughing.

"That man has a wife."

"So."

"So. You can't be his woman." She waved me off and I ran up on her.

"Beat her ass." Cecily was yelling out. I kept fucking Shayla up.

"Hurry up Rebel. We were supposed to be in and out."

"You got your gun on you?" She pulled it out the garter belt under her dress.

"Turn the TV up." She didn't have a silencer on it and we couldn't take the chance of anyone hearing. It would fuck the entire plan up. Once it was loud, I covered her face with a pillow and blew her fucking brains out. Blood was over the walls and on the floor. I stood up, ran in the bathroom and washed the blood off my hands.

"Let's go." We closed the door behind us and went in search of Sway. We couldn't find him, so I had her call. He was in some room on the other side of the house. I opened the door and he had a big ass smile on his face.

"Thanks, so much Cecily for bringing my cousin. Can you excuse us for a minute?" I nodded my head for her to go. I knew she was only going to stand outside.

"Where you been Rebel?" He got up off the bed and came over to me.

"Sway, I told you I wasn't working for you anymore, after Shayla shot me."

"And I told you, its over when I say it is."

WHAP! WHAP! My face turned with each smack. I swear, I didn't miss this part of the job.

"What do you want Sway? You had Cecily bring me here under false pretenses. You must want something."

"I want you to kill Cason and Pierce." I threw my head back laughing."

"Bitch, ain't shit funny." He smacked me again and this time, I felt my lip bust open.

"Sway, you have one more time to hit me and I promise you'll regret it."

"Bitch, please. There's no competition." He pushed me on the bed and stood in front of me.

"Move Sway."

"Nah. You wanna be out here giving my pussy away, I'm gonna have to remind you, of who you really belong to."

"I belong to my fiancé and he's the only one who will touch this pussy." When I saw him remove his jeans, I knew there would be no way for me to get outta this. Sway is a big dude and if he's aggressive, nothing I do will work. I pretended to unbutton my clothes and pressed the button.

BOOM! BOOM!

"What is that?"

"Niggas downstairs being stupid. Now lay back."

"No Sway. This is not happening."

"Oh, you're giving up the pussy." He backhanded me and my entire body fell on the bed. My nose was gushing out blood. He started fumbling with my pants and that's when the door flew open.

"I wish you would touching my fucking wife." Pierce's voice was just what I needed to hear. I rolled off the bed and ran in the bathroom. Sway, had his hands up.

"CECILY, GET MY GIRL OUTTA HERE!" He shouted and I kicked Sway in the dick on the way out.

"Get down Rebel." Gunfire was going off, all through the house. Bodies were sprawled out and the women were screaming.

"You good?" Alex asked.

"Yea."

"Cecily, take her to the blue truck. They have medical equipment in there." He went past us, in the house.

Once we got to the truck, I'll be damned if it didn't look like a small doctor's office. Who are these motherfuckers? I thought Cason and Pierce were crazy but these niggas are worse. I noticed all the guys walking out and not even three minutes later, the entire house exploded. I shook my head and let the guy check me out. He said, my nose wasn't broken but its going to cause black eyes. I rather that, then to walk around with a big ass nose splint.

"Fuck! Rebel, you should've told us to come in sooner." Pierce examined my face.

"I'm fine."

"How the fuck am I supposed to fuck you with a beat-up face? That shit looks crazy." Cecily started laughing.

"Please don't entertain him."

"I can't help it. My bad."

"Lets go. I'll have to either fuck you in total darkness or only from behind. This shit is ridiculous." I had to laugh at how mad he got.

"I love you Pierce." I leaned over to kiss him.

"I love you too ma. Can you still suck my dick with black eyes and a swollen nose?"

"Ughhhhh. You make me sick." He kissed me on the lips and I rode off into the sunset with my man.

The End...

CPSIA information can be obtained
at www.ICGtesting.com
Printed in the USA
LVHW081250190119
604507LV00041B/1047/P